City of Death

RICHARD JAMES

This edition published in 2020 by Sharpe Books

Table of Contents

The following two short stories take place after the events of the first novel in the Bowman Of The Yard series, THE HEAD IN THE ICE.

CITY OF DEATH

THE SMITHFIELD MURDER

FEBRUARY, 1892

Archie Walton hated these February mornings. In all his eleven years he'd never known hardship like it. As all around him the city slept, he was obliged to eschew his bed and open the trader's stall held by his master at Smithfield Market. On account of a clear night sky, tonight felt especially cold. His eyes stung as he blinked into the freezing air. Already his fingers were numb. As he walked away from the Thames up Old Bailey, he looked around him at the buildings. Newgate Prison stood imperious and forbidding, as if in warning. Behind, the dome of St Paul's dared show itself on the skyline. The road narrowed as he approached St. Sepulchre's church, and already he could hear the squawking and swearing of the early traders at Smithfield. Archie had been in the church just once. He had filched some apples from a street stall last summer, and found himself on the wrong end of a Peeler's wrath. Giving a holler, the constable gave chase, his hobnailed boots skidding on the streets beneath him. Archie was young and fast and had soon left his pursuer behind on Hosier Street. He had taken sanctuary amongst St. Sepulchre's broad, uncluttered interior and wide supporting pillars. As he took the time to catch his breath, he had allowed his eyes to wander to the church's broad, coffered ceiling. A series of vaults and arches held the great roof aloft. A pattern of sunken square panels led the eye to the centre of a dome. There, as the light of a summer's day had bled through the stained glass, Archie ate his apple. He walked to the chancel and let his hand run across the altar. The wood had felt alive and warm to the touch. As he spat pips to the floor, Archie took a final look around. If the majesty of St. Sepulchre's had made any impression at all on his young mind, he didn't show it. His feast concluded, he had simply wiped his mouth on a sleeve, allowed himself a chuckle at the afternoon's events and made his way out through the transept door. That summer's day seemed a long time ago now. Archie shivered to his core as he made his way round the church onto Snow Hill. The bell chimed twice from its tower, heralding his arrival at the market on his appointed hour.

Before him, there was a circus of activity. The hustle and bustle seemed quite at odds with the early hour. The grand, vaulted entrance was crammed with carts and drays, each disgorging themselves of their loads into the waiting arms of butchers and traders. Great sides of beef were heaved onto shoulders. Cuts of pork were passed aloft from man to man. Geese, chickens and rarer fowl were slung over arms and carried gracelessly through the iron arches at the market's entrance. Livestock was shepherded in from their carts to be shown at their best in the hope of a sale. Nearing the entrance hall to the ostentatiously named Grand Avenue, the sweet, ripe odour of raw meat and manure pricked at Archie's nostrils. He shouldered his way through the throng, stepping this way and that across a curious dance floor. Each man embraced his load as a partner, waltzing his way to his allotted stall. Cleavers fell and knives struck. The air was rent with the rasp of saw on bone. Cattle that had been driven through the streets of London were herded to their pens, chickens clucked from their crates and pigs bedded down in their straw. Kicking through the sawdust at his feet, Archie found himself at his stall at last. Blowing on his fingers to restore some feeling, he reached into a pocket for his keys. He had been entrusted with them by his master.

Solomon Hibbert was always late. He had held his place in the market for forty years and felt his longevity alone entitled him to certain liberties. Being late for the morning's work was one of them. He had taken Archie on just a year previously. Taking a young lad from a poor house and putting him to work chimed with Hibbert's ideals. Paying him a pittance chimed with them even more. It was Archie's job to open the stall, direct the deliveries and await the arrival of his master. If he was lucky, he'd get a penny for his pains or a sausage to throw on the brazier beneath Holborn Viaduct. Archie pulled up the shutter with a clatter. The lamps in the hall barely penetrated the gloom within.

'Shift yer arse, boy!' Archie turned to see a thickset man with a haunch of beef at his shoulder. He rolled a cigarette between his teeth. 'Or I'll drop this on yer 'ead like a ton of bricks.' He slammed the carcass on the block in Hibbert's stall, wiping blood from his hands with his apron. 'Foreman'll be round in a minute for payment.'

Dropping ash to the floor, the man returned to his cart at the market's entrance, ready to shoulder another burden in the name of commerce. Archie rolled his eyes. Stamping his feet against the cold, he turned his attention to the meat on the block. Room would have to be made. Pausing only to light a lamp on the wall, he crept to the back of the stall where it was due to hang. A rail ran the length of the right hand wall, some eight feet from the ground. It was crammed with sides of pork, haunches of beef and lambs wrapped in muslin cloth, all suspended on hooks, and all to be sold in the next three days. Hibbert was overreaching himself again. Bracing himself against the first carcass, Archie leaned against it to give it a hefty push. The meat swung back an inch or two then came to a stubborn halt on the rail. It had snagged. He pressed his shoulder to the animal, trying again. Still it stayed resolutely where it hung. Muttering under his breath, Archie grabbed a wooden stool from the counter and dragged it through the sawdust to the rail. If he could make room for the beef on the rail, Hibbert could lift it up on his arrival. Shifting his weight on the stool, Archie stretched up, feeling with his fingers where the snag might be. He felt nothing. Leaning against the side of pork to his left, he felt the blockage was behind it. Giving it a push, he unbalanced himself and fell to the floor. A peel of laughter rang out behind him and Archie turned to see a passing tradesman with a string of sausages about his neck. 'Best laugh I've 'ad all mornin','' he chuckled. As the man passed on about his errand, Archie looked up and behind the side of pork that had defeated him. There, some three feet from the ground, hung a pair of feet. Panicking, Archie grabbed the side of pork and swung it towards the front of the rail. It revealed a spectacle so grisly that the boy was suddenly lost for breath. Looking up beyond the feet, he saw a slick of blood had dried on the unfortunate man's legs. His arms hung limp at his side, his chin resting incongruously on his chest as though he were simply asleep. Archie's hand went involuntarily to his mouth. There before him, hung Solomon Hibbert.

'How the devil did you know I'd be here?' Detective Inspector Ignatius Hicks sat at the fireplace in The Silver Cross Inn, a look of incredulity on his face. His hat lay on the table before him, next to a steaming plate of kippers and a tankard of ale. He was clearly irritated at the interruption to his breakfast.

'A lucky hunch?' sparkled Anthony Graves from the door. The sergeant was his usual ebullient self. Inspector Bowman marveled that, even on this coldest of mornings, his companion had refused to wear a hat. They had been despatched from Scotland Yard and instructed to pick up Inspector Hicks on their way.

'You're to accompany us to Smithfield,' Bowman growled.

'They've found an unexpected carcass at the meat market.' Graves gave Hicks the flash of a smile. Bowman, not for the first time, marveled at how his colleague could find such sport in something so grim.

'Smithfield?' Hicks roared loud enough to wake the

landlord from his stupor at the bar. 'I can't go to Smithfield at this hour. Think of my constitution.'

'Your constitution?' Bowman raised his eyes to the heavens as if in silent prayer.

Hicks had leaned forward conspiratorially. If he knew he was brushing his kippers with the ends of his beard, he didn't seem to care. 'I suffer terribly with the gas,' he elucidated in hushed tones. 'To see such sights as they have at Smithfield would be enough to turn a man's stomach.'

Bowman's moustache twitched at his mouth in irritation. 'I would think such a man as could stomach kippers at this hour could stomach anything.'

Hicks threw him a look of reproach. 'I have a delicate digestion, Bowman, and that is that.' He tried not to react to the sudden delivery of a large pile of devilled eggs at his elbow. Bowman stared at the portly inspector, his eyebrows raised almost to the brim of his hat. 'Eggs help,' Hicks offered, meekly.

'Sergeant Graves, would you be so good as to settle the inspector's tab at the bar?' Bowman turned on his heels to head for the door. 'Time is of the essence.'

Reluctantly, Hicks delved into a pocket to retrieve some change for Graves. As he leaned over to take Hicks' payment, the young sergeant plucked an egg from his plate with a cheery wink.

'Why is there need for so many of us?' Hicks implored, shrugging on his coat.

'We'll need numbers to keep the crowds at bay,'

Bowman explained. 'The market is about to get busy.'

'Boothby,' announced the market manager in his flat, northern vowels. 'Arthur Boothby'. He was an officious-looking man, marked Bowman as he shook his hand. A large, white apron was tied at his waist to protect the full tweed suit he wore beneath. A cap balanced precariously on his head, beneath which jutted a pair of particularly bushy brows. His nose was flat and wide as if the result of some past altercation, and his mouth was thin and perpetually pursed in a look of disdain. A leather pouch at his side bulged with papers. Bowman took the opportunity to glance around.

Smithfield Market was truly a cathedral to the carnivore. It seemed as tall as one of Brunel's greatest stations, and no less ornate. The ubiquitous London pigeon had made its home amongst the great girders that spanned the entire length of the roof and a network of glass, wood and steel gave out to a still dark sky. The horizon, noticed Bowman, was painted with paler colours and he fancied he could sense the imminent arrival of the morning sun.

'Looks like our Solomon has gone the way of William Wallace,' Boothby was saying.

'How's that?' Graves asked, nonplussed, his clear blue eyes clouded with confusion.

'Smithfield is the site of the old Tyburn tree. You might well be standing where William Wallace swung from the gallows. Aye, and Wat Tyler, too.'

Everywhere Bowman looked, he saw flesh of every sort, plucked, rolled and stuffed for consumption. Buckets of offal littered the floor, cuts of meat hung at every stall. Pig's heads were displayed with no little ceremony amongst cuts of lamb and guinea fowl. The fetid air mixed with the smell of tobacco from Hicks' habitual pipe which he held tight in his teeth as if it were a prize. Bowman resisted the urge to retch. Catching Hicks' eye he affected a more nonchalant air. The last thing he wanted was to show weakness to his bluff companion. The affair with the severed head in the ice had cost him dear, both in terms of his own sanity, but also with his standing in the Force. Bowman was becoming used to the sideways glances and whispers behind hands, but he could not bear to be exposed to Hicks.

Swallowing hard, he continued. 'Mr Boothby,' he soothed, 'we are here to investigate the death of Solomon Hibbert. Whilst the history lesson is engaging, it would be of greater benefit to us if we could see the body.'

With a barely contained snort of disappointment, Boothby adjusted the cap on his head and turned about. 'Number thirty-four,' he barked. 'That's where you'll find him. And I'll thank you to be quick. We open in twenty minutes and I won't turn trade away.'

'How are you bearing up, Hicks?' teased Graves as they walked through the great iron arch at the market's entrance.

'Tolerably,' Hicks mumbled, picking errant scraps of kipper from his beard.

Ahead of them, the great hall was split into avenues of stalls that stretched as far as the eye could see to the left and right. Shutters were thrown open in anticipation of the day's custom, stalls were laden with produce, boys mopped the floors with steaming water and blocks were scrubbed and scraped.

Arthur Boothby was warming to his theme as they approached stall number thirty-four. 'Seven hundred years ago, you'd be walking amongst the throng of Bartholomew Fair,' he expounded. 'We like to think we're following in illustrious footsteps.'

Inspector Hicks cast a glance around him. 'Though perhaps with fewer freaks and wire-walkers,' he offered.

Conscious that his other companions were only feigning interest at best, Boothby stopped and cleared his throat. 'Stall number thirty-four,' he announced, gesturing towards where a young boy sat on a stool. The boy regarded the assembled inspectors with doleful eyes. 'This is the lad that found him,' Boothby explained. 'And there is the man himself.' With more drama than Bowman felt strictly necessary, Boothby lifted an arm to point grandly up at the rail.

Inspector Bowman fought the urge to vomit. Solomon Hibbert was held suspended by a meat hook through the back of his neck. Bowman could plainly see the point of the hook protruding through the man's Adam's apple. His entire torso was caked in a sheen of blood which dripped down his arms and onto his fingers. Casting his eyes to the floor, Bowman could see Solomon's blood mixing with the sawdust. Sergeant Graves was standing next to the body now, prodding it almost playfully with his fingers.

'Has anything been moved?' Bowman asked of

Boothby.

'No one has approached the body. Save the boy who found him, of course. I think his name is Archie.'

Sergeant Graves had sidled up to the inspector, lowering his voice in the throng. 'Look around you, sir.'

Bowman did just that. 'I see nothing Graves, just people going about their business.' Hawkers were filling the aisles with produce for sale; pies and pasties, raw meats and offal. Traders argued over prices while competing stallholders gazed with envious eyes at their neighbour's displays. 'There's nothing out of the ordinary.'

'Precisely, sir.' Graves gave a knowing look. 'Three inspectors have just arrived from Scotland Yard to investigate a body found hanging on a meat hook. And no one seems to be the least bit concerned.' He cast a sad look at the ruffian on the stool. 'They've not even seen fit to comfort the boy.'

Graves was right. Aside from some sidelong glances and knowing nudges between the stallholders, their arrival had passed without interest.

'What does that tell us?' Bowman asked.

'That he had no friends here?' Graves offered, brightly.

Bowman nodded. 'Inspector Hicks, speak to these men. I want to know more about Solomon Hibbert. What of his character? Did they have any dealings with the man?'

Boothby gave a snort of derision. 'I wish you luck in finding any man that had a good word for him.'

Inspector Hicks pulled himself up to his full height. 'Perhaps, Mr Boothby, I should start with you. Might I trouble you to tell me all you know of the deceased?'

Boothby gave an obsequious tip of his head. 'Aye, you might. But I'd rather do it beyond the sight of the traders. You can accompany me to my office.'

'Excellent,' Hicks smacked his lips. 'Then perhaps I might avail myself of a pasty on the way.'

Seemingly pleased to meet a kindred spirit, Boothby allowed himself a smile. Alarmingly, he exposed the greatest display of crooked teeth that Bowman had ever seen. 'Oh, and inspector,' Boothby turned to face Bowman as he left. 'You will appreciate that we open for business at seven of the clock. I would not wish our customers to face such a sight.' He cast a look of distaste in the direction of Hibbert's body. 'Such a thing might put them off their purchases.' He gave a ghastly wink. 'And we all have debts to pay.'

As Hicks led the man away, Bowman heard them fall into easy conversation concerning the variety of meats available and the favourable terms that might be met for a man who wished to purchase them while in the company of the market manager.

'Graves,' barked Bowman irritably. 'Get that man down.'

While Graves made it his business to raise a working party from the traders about him, Bowman approached the lad on the stool. Archie Walton looked up as the inspector crouched beside him, his coat tails trailing in the sawdust. He had a haunted look, thought the boy. Troubled.

'What will I do for work?' Archie asked, plaintively.

'Some other of the traders will employ you,' Bowman

offered, absently smoothing his moustache between his fingers.

The boy looked sadly about him. 'He was not liked,' he said quietly. 'And nor am I.'

'Who would have keys to this stall, Archie?'

'Only me and Mr Boothby.'

'Hibbert trusted you with his key?'

The boy nodded. 'So I could open up.'

'And when was the last time you saw Mr Hibbert?'

'Yesterday at midday. He gave me a sausage for the journey home. I cooked it with the tramps under the viaduct.'

'So he was good to you?'

'Better than he was to his wife.'

Bowman's eyes flashed wide. 'I'll pay no heed to gossip, boy.'

'Everyone knows it. He beat her somethin' rotten when he was in his cups.'

A sudden thought occurred to the inspector as he rose. 'Has she been told?' The boy shrugged with indifference. It was plain he neither knew nor cared. With a sigh, Bowman looked about him, wondering how best to proceed. Hicks had begun his interviews and Graves was busy at the rail. Three burly men had reluctantly been pressed into lowering Hibbert's body. By resting its weight on their shoulders they were attempting to lift it off its hook and onto the floor. Bowman let his gaze wander to the ground. Absentmindedly wiping his coat tails free of sawdust, an idea came to him.

'Wait!' he commanded. The note of authority in his

voice was enough to stop the men in their tracks.

Graves turned to face him, a look of enquiry in his bright, blue eyes. 'Sir?'

'Step back from the body,' Bowman ordered, his face a mask of concentration.

The three men stepped back, bemused. Inspector Bowman was circling the body, looking all around at the man's feet, legs and torso.

'Archie, when was this sawdust laid out?'

'Put it out meself before I left yesterday,' Archie said simply. 'I do it every day.'

Bowman looked his fellow detective up and down, then turned his gaze to the men he had enlisted. 'We all have sawdust on our clothing, Graves. You and I have been here a matter of minutes, and yet there is sawdust on my coat and on the hems of your trousers. You even have some in your hair.'

'Gets everywhere,' pronounced one of the men in a strong cockney accent.

'Perks of the job,' offered the other with a laugh.

'Plainly.' Bowman was frowning again. 'And yet Mr Hibbert has not a speck upon him.'

The two men were silenced, the smiles frozen upon their faces. Their eyes fell upon Hibbert's body. Sergeant Graves was walking all around him now. 'What does it mean?'

Bowman had thrust his hands deep in his pockets. 'It means,' he began, 'that Mr Hibbert was killed elsewhere, carried here then hung up with his wares.'

Alice Hibbert had once been a beauty. Looking from her clear, sparkling eyes to her even clearer skin, Bowman could see that perhaps only a few years before, she would have turned many an admiring head. Her steel grey hair was pinned up, secured with a glittering clip in the shape of a butterfly. She was dressed conservatively in a frilled dress and sat, demurely, with her hands clasped at her lap. Looking about him, Bowman's gaze was drawn to an ornate clock at the mantelpiece. It was framed on a plinth of green marble, its numerals etched in a dark Arabic text. It stood proudly amongst some other trinkets; an ostentatious picture frame decorated in fine gold filigree, a representation in china of a skating couple. The paneled walls around the room were inlaid with a floral print, punctuated periodically by tasteful landscapes. A fire blazed in the grate, dispelling the morning cold with a fierce heat. If it hadn't been for the purple bruise that adorned her cheek, Mrs Hibbert would have offered the perfect picture of domestic bliss. Bowman swallowed hard and waited. The woman stared at him, her voice caught in her throat.

'Are you sure?' she whispered, barely audible above the crackling of the fire. 'Are you sure it's him?' Her voice had an Irish lilt that, even in these circumstances, Bowman found appealing.

The inspector nodded. 'His boy found him.' He had spared her the details. It was enough for her to know that Solomon Hibbert was dead. The manner of his death could follow in due course. Her hands were shaking now, and she lifted them to her face. Her eyes creased in an effort to contain her feelings and Bowman found himself wincing in anticipation. And then she did the last thing he had expected. She laughed. Rocking back in her chair, it was as if some great relief had come to her.

'Mrs Hibbert,' he began, confused, 'I'm not certain you understand the implications - '

'So the bastard is dead. Well, he had it coming.' She took a breath and sighed. 'You must forgive me, inspector, but if anyone deserved a drubbing, it was Solomon Hibbert.'

Bowman turned his hat in his hands. He had heard stories of such women from his own wife, Anna. She had taken work with the Salvation Army in Hanbury Street and would often talk of the cases that presented themselves. Women who were beaten by their husbands like dogs, others who were thrown out of house and home with nothing to their name. Such men were often drunk, sometimes mad, and rarely punished. Marriage was considered a private affair and many a man felt free to use his wife as he wished.

'Do you have a wife, Inspector Bowman?'

The question brought him up short. She was the first to ask since his release from the asylum. The first to ask since Anna had died. He was unsure how to answer. Did he have a wife? Bowman felt his face flush. He swallowed hard. Blinking away a memory of Anna on their wedding day, he turned to Alice Hibbert.

'Yes,' he replied simply. It was not the response he had

thought to give. 'Yes, I have a wife.'

'And a fine husband I'm sure you make.' Alice's eyes sought Bowman's, as if some understanding might be found there. 'But not all men are the same.' She had risen now, and walked to the mantelpiece. Warming her hands at the fire, she turned to face the inspector. 'My husband was a brute,' she said boldly, her chin jutting forward in defiance. 'And I hated him.'

'Mrs Hibbert, would you know of anyone who might want to see your husband dead?' Bowman sensed the ridiculous nature of the question even as he asked it.

Alice threw back her head and laughed again; a full-throated laugh, released without care. 'It might be quicker to make a list of those who would want him still alive.'

'When was the last time you were in his company, Mrs Hibbert?'

Alice thought. 'Last night, inspector. He spent the evening asleep in that very chair until the clock struck eight. Then he sprang from the chair and ran from the house. As he does every week at that time.'

'He does the same thing every week? He leaves the house at eight o'clock?'

'Every Wednesday,' Alice confirmed. 'To see a man about a dog, he would say.' Her soft Irish lilt rendered the phrase all the more charming. 'And then an hour later he'd return with money in his fist. Except, last night, he never returned at all.' Bowman raised a quizzical eyebrow. 'There is a loose tile at my feet, inspector. It conceals a hole where you may find a tin box, locked with a key. It's where he kept his notes. He was never one to trust his money to a bank.'

'May I see?' Bowman leaned forward where he sat, his eyes searching the hearth for the very tile.

Alice Hibbert seemed to weigh the question in her mind. 'I will happily show you the box and its contents, Inspector Bowman, but I would ask that you look away while I retrieve it.'

Bowman turned his back to the fire. As his eyes focused on a picture of a pastoral scene before him, he heard the scraping of brickwork at his back. The tile lifted, the widow bade him turn. She held a tin box some twelve inches long and six deep. He was surprised to see the lid already open on its hinges.

'He allowed you access to the box?' he enquired.

'I keep the key about my neck,' Alice replied, holding it aloft on its chain so that he may see. 'I was free to take as much and as often as I saw fit. Solomon kept me well so I wanted for little. I rarely had recourse to take his money.'

'But did it never occur to you - '

'To leave, inspector?' she interrupted. 'I had the means, certainly. Such a man has a hold over a woman you would not understand. Why does a beaten dog not run?'

'Because he is afraid,' Bowman nodded in sympathy.

'Quite right, inspector. Afraid of being caught.' She held the box forward so that Bowman could see its contents. There were notes of practically every denomination held within.

'There must be a hundred pounds,' he gasped. Half what a detective might expect to earn in a year.

'Very likely,' Alice conceded, snapping the lid shut.

'Look about you, inspector. I live a comfortable life, my every whim is catered for. These trinkets and baubles,' she waved a hand at the ornaments on the mantle and the pictures on the wall, 'Are merely reparations.' She smiled at Bowman's questioning look. 'To assuage him of his guilt. The more he beat me, the better gifts he would bring. It helped him, I suppose.'

Bowman felt his anger rising. How could marriage be held in such low regard by some, when he had been denied its gifts? He bit his lip. 'Where did his money come from?' The inspector doubted a humble butcher could bring home such a wage.

'You think I would ask?' Alice Hibbert's eyes scolded him. 'You cannot comprehend of a life with Solomon Hibbert. To ask him anything would be to risk his wrath.' Bowman felt chastened under her gaze and rose to leave.

'I would ask you, Mrs Hibbert, to report to me anything you might think to be of use in my investigations.'

'Investigate all you want, Inspector Bowman,' She was seeing him to the door now. 'And if you find him, bring the murderer to me that I might shake his hand.'

Hibbert's body lay face down on the butcher's block. As Bowman approached, Graves ran towards him, waving his arms in alarm.

'Hicks has opened the market!' he yelled. Bowman quickened his step to join his companion. 'Boothby's charmed him, now Hicks has acquiesced. There's a hundred people at the gates, all champing at the bit to get in.' Graves' curls bounced on his head in agitation and his face was flushed with concern.

'We can't have people tramping through this market,' seethed Bowman, 'while we are in the midst of an investigation. Where is Hicks?'

His question was answered by the appearance of the inspector himself. Hicks was carrying himself at full stretch, his chest puffed out in direct challenge to Bowman. 'Worry not, inspector,' he began. 'I have arranged for the removal of the body on a cart. There is no reason to delay the prospect of a day's living to these unfortunate souls.' Hicks gestured widely to indicate the traders and sellers who milled about him. 'They can't all be guilty of murder.'

Bowman was fuming. 'Inspector Hicks,' he spat. 'You should know that you are here against my better judgment. If it were not for the commissioner's insistence, you would still be scoffing eggs at the inn.'

Hicks' eyes were wide with incredulity. 'Where was your precious judgement on Lambeth Bridge, Inspector Bowman?' Bowman was taken aback at the remark. He stole a glance to Graves who could not meet his gaze. So, he had been talking.

'What do you know of Lambeth Bridge?' Bowman felt his face flush against the cold morning air. He was fighting hard not to swallow.

Hicks looked directly at his fellow inspector. 'I know what I know,' he said unflinchingly. Bowman blinked. The events on Lambeth Bridge seemed a lifetime away. It came as some surprise that they had only happened four weeks since. 'Now,' continued Hicks gruffly, 'I will have that body moved and I will open this market.' He reached beneath the folds of his great coat and, almost improbably, retrieved a ledger. 'In the meantime,' he teased, 'I will leave you with this. It is from Boothby's office and contains a list of every man to be employed here. I've had my fill of intrigue for the day.' He thrust the book into Bowman's hands and retreated through the throng. With a pipe between his teeth and a spring in his step, Hicks had every intention of spending the rest of the day at The Silver Cross.

It took four men to lift Hibbert's body and lower it onto the cart. With the block now clear of its grisly burden, Bowman placed the book upon it. 'Where do we start, Graves? There must be over two hundred names here. And who's to say the killer is amongst them?'

Graves threw him a cheery look. 'It's a start though, isn't it, sir?'

Bowman studied his companion. He had thought Graves dependable. A friend, perhaps. Bowman supposed it only natural that he should have been talking. The inspector had almost frustrated the investigation into the head in the ice. But for a moment of clarity, the end might very well have been different. He had not been himself. He knew that now, and wondered whether he would ever be himself again. 'Yes, Graves, it's a start. Have a word with Boothby, would you? Get those gates closed again so we can proceed, ask him of his whereabouts last night, then direct your attention to the stall holders along this row.'

Sergeant Graves nodded his assent, turning away to

Boothby's office while Bowman closed the pages to the ledger. It made sense, he thought, to interview those traders directly adjacent to number thirty-four to begin with. Hibbert's immediate neighbours struck the inspector as an unlikely pairing. The older of the two, a man who introduced himself as O'Sheehy, was a middle-aged man of Irish stock. A shock of ginger-red hair was barely contained beneath a bowler hat, his wide girth strained against his blood-stained apron. A pipe clamped between his teeth, O'Sheehy regarded Bowman with suspicion.

'I had nothing to do with the man if I could help it. He was a drunk,' O'Sheehy sniffed. 'He went about his business and I went about mine.'

He was joined by a much younger, wiry man with a pockmarked face. He stood with his hands in his pockets as he looked Bowman up and down. 'I wouldn't give him the time of day if his life depended on it,' he drawled.

'And where were you last night, when Hibbert was killed?' Bowman licked the stub of his pencil, ready to record such information as the two traders would deign to give him.

'With Boothby. At The Bishop's Finger across the way,' O'Sheehy pointed beyond the market entrance to the street beyond. 'We need a pint or two to get us fettled before we put ourselves to bed.'

Bowman made a note and looked to O'Sheehy's companion. The younger man looked the inspector straight in the eye. 'We often head there after a day at the market.'

'Were you in company?' Bowman asked.

'Aye,' confirmed the older man, filling his pipe with fresh tobacco from a pouch. 'With a good many of those you see around us. Until the bell was rung and we were sent to our homes. If Gladstone hadn't had his way we'd still be there now.' The two men shared the joke, O'Sheehy jabbing his companion in the ribs with an elbow.

Bowman sighed. William Gladstone had believed alcohol to be the curse of the working man. To curb his excesses, he had enacted a Bill while Prime Minister to close public houses in the towns and cities at midnight.

'Then you had but two hours' sleep?' Bowman's raised eyebrow was enough to betray his scepticism.

'Does no harm once a week,' O'Sheehy proclaimed, airily. 'We don't keep Scotland Yard hours here, inspector.' His eyes narrowed. 'We work hard and we play hard.'

As a preliminary interview, it had yielded nothing. Bowman nodded in understanding, tipping his hat in thanks as he snapped his notebook shut. With an impending sense of futility, he moved to the next stall. He was confronted by a frail looking man with mean eyes and a shifty countenance. He introduced himself as Griffiths and retold the same story almost word for word.

'I closed the stall as the bells struck four, inspector,' his voice had a nasal quality to it which under other circumstances could have been described as comical. 'Not a minute later. I know there are some here who will stay to mop up the dregs of custom but, as I always say, a day's work is a day's work.' Bowman couldn't help but agree, pencil poised for anything of import. 'I passed Hibbert on my way out. I said nothing to him,' Griffiths' voice rose as if in anticipation of a dramatic climax. 'And he said nothing to me.' He folded his arms, in the clear hope of saying nothing more.

'And then?' asked Bowman.

Quite predictably, the man lifted a bony digit to point beyond the market's entrance. 'I had an evening at The Bishop's Finger with Boothby. Me and a few others here go way back with him. Ask around, inspector, you'll find I was in good company. We sometimes need a pint or two to get us fettled after a busy day.' He threw Bowman a defiant look. It was plain he considered the interview to be at an end.

Bowman suspected that every trader in the market would tell the same tale. He was happy to be disabused of the notion at the next stall along. The young man at the counter was busy at his trade. A sharp knife was brought to bear on a cut of beef. Bowman took the time to stand and watch the youth at his work. With expert skill, he cut around the bones, removing them without a trace of meat attached. The resulting joint was rolled and skewered, with a layer of fat held in place with string.

'Fine work,' Bowman offered in admiration.

The young man lifted his gaze to meet the inspector. He was the first of the traders to offer his hand in greeting. Bowman felt he should reciprocate.

'Stanley Kelley,' the man announced, pointing with his

free hand to an ornate sign above his stall. There his name was emblazoned, along with the legend 'A Butcher To Trust'.

Reaching for his notebook, Bowman paused with his hand in his pocket. Perhaps it might be better to just converse with the man. 'Been here long?' he enquired.

'Since Christmas,' Kelley replied, carrying the joint of beef to a shelf. 'It was busy enough but a butcher's trade is not a way to get rich.' He lay a leg of lamb upon the block and set about it with a cleaver. 'I'm hoping you'll get this market open soon so I can make enough to keep a family.'

'You have children?' The man was clearly older than he looked.

'Three of the blighters.' Despite the tone in his voice, Kelley's eyes lit up as he spoke of them. 'The oldest, Molly, she's five now. Then I have twins of two years old. They'd eat all the contents of my stall if I let 'em.' He winked at the inspector, a charming smile bringing colour to his cheeks. 'And I probably would.'

'You take pride in your work, I see.'

Kelley was wiping his hands on his apron. 'Couldn't face me missus if I didn't. She's with the bairns all day, bless her. I couldn't go home to her at nights if I'd spent the day skiving.'

Bowman couldn't help but smile. Every now and then, but rarely, he would meet a man or woman in the course of his duties who restored a faith in humanity. Heaven knows he needed it. Stanley Kelley was just such a man, and all the more welcome in this investigation for it. 'The

Empire would be a better place with more like you at its vanguard, Kelley.'

Kelley's eyes lit up at the remark. 'I'd agree with that, inspector. There are too many men content to sit back and play the country for a fool.' He leaned in conspiratorially, lowering his voice almost to a whisper. 'There are many here to whom I would ascribe such behaviour. Men who are not afraid to break the law for a profit.' He moved back to his block again, sharpening his blade on a stone. 'Not me, inspector. Sweat and hard work will see us through,' he was back at his work again, deftly slicing meat from the bone before him. 'And put meat on my table, too.'

'Could you tell me where you were last night?'

'I was where you'll find me every night. In the warmth of my own bed with my family about me.'

Bowman nodded in thanks and looked about him. Perhaps Graves was having better luck. Whistling through his teeth in exasperation, Bowman returned to Hibbert's stall to look through the ledger. There were over a hundred stalls numbered in its greasy pages. His heart sank at the thought of addressing every man inside them. If Hicks had still been here he could have sent back to the Yard for manpower. He made a mental note to reprimand the man upon his return. Looking up, he saw Sergeant Graves approaching. He was shaking his head in despair.

'This is like a labour of Hercules. If truth be told, I'd rather be tasked with catching the Cretan Bull than taking statements from every man here.'

'Agreed,' concurred Bowman sadly.

'And if I hear the word 'fettled' once more,' continued

Graves, frustrated, 'I shall not be responsible for my actions.' The sentiment was all the more surprising given Graves' usually cheerful disposition.

'You heard that, too?'

Graves nodded. 'I'd never known the word before, yet I've heard it four times in the last forty minutes. Heaven alone knows what it means.'

Bowman lifted his hat to smooth his troubled brow with the back of a hand. 'They've been schooled by someone.'

'Why?' Graves looked around him, suddenly seeing the market and its traders in a new light.

'There's a young man in stall number thirty-one,' Bowman traced his finger along the names in the ledger. 'Stanley Kelley.' He tapped the name in the book. 'He seemed to suggest there are those amongst the traders who are not as honest as they could be. Perhaps Solomon Hibbert was one of the worst.'

Turning from Hibbert's stall, Bowman's attention was drawn to the steps by the market entrance. He was presented with a doleful sight. There sat Archie Walton, the young butcher's boy who had found his master on the hook that morning.

'He's got nothing, sir.' Graves cast a saddened look in the boy's direction. 'And no other traders will touch him.'

'Where will he go?' Bowman's moustache was twitching. It seemed to him that Archie was an incidental casualty of the night's events. The inspector felt sorry for him.

'The street?' suggested Graves, matter-of-factly.

Bowman thought for a moment. 'Sergeant Graves, I'm

going to The Bishop's Finger to speak with whomsoever I can concerning these men's stories. I'm of a mind to take him with me for a plate of eels. How would that please him, do you think?'

A wide smile spread all over Graves' face as he considered the proposition. 'I should imagine it would please him greatly,' he beamed.

The Bishop's Finger stood not even a stone's throw from the market. Crossing the road at West Smithfield, Archie Walton could barely contain his excitement. It was an airy, welcoming establishment with an ornate bar and a fine selection of ales. As the two men sat at a table by the window with their charge, an order was made for two jars of ale and a plate of jellied eels.

'Take us through your day, Archie.' Bowman was leaning forward, one hand on Boothby's ledger as the boy ate.

'I open the stall at the stroke of two. Never early, never late. The carts are there by then and I show the men where the stock should go. They'd leave it on the block more often as not and Hibbert would hang it when he arrived.'

'What time would that be?'

'Always on the half hour.'

'Why so?' Graves took a sip from his jar, leaving a moustache of foam on his upper lip.

'He reckoned havin' been so long at his trade, he had earned an extra half hour in bed. Can I ask you a question now, inspector?'

Bowman shared a look with his companion. The boy had

spirit.

'Anything.' Bowman spread his hands wide in supplication.

'What did the other inspector mean by talking of Lambeth Bridge?'

Graves spluttered on his beer. Bowman suddenly felt very hot. Pulling at his collar with his fingers, he swallowed hard. Of course, Archie had been mere feet away during his altercation with Hicks at the market. He chose to ignore the question. 'Graves, would you call the barmaid over? Let's see if she remembers anything of her customers last night.'

Grateful for the diversion, Graves looked around. He fixed on a comely woman cleaning glasses at the bar. Her hair was heaped up on her head, a pinafore tied tight around her waist serving only to accentuate her generous shape. He downed the last of his beer and wiped his mouth salaciously on the back of his hand. Eyes gleaming, he swaggered to the bar to engage the lady in conversation. Ignoring Archie's look of confusion, Bowman went on.

'The market opens at seven o'clock. What would you do for those five hours?'

'Hibbert would cut and saw the meat.' Alfie slurped on his eels, spooning the liquor into his eager mouth as he talked. 'I'd dress it for the counter, mop the floor and scrub the block. Sometimes run errands.'

'Until noon, when you would be let go?'

'And I'd be in me bed by ten minutes past. That'd be me done in for the day.'

'Where do you live, Archie?' Bowman leaned back from

the table.

'Limeburner Lane. Me and me sister found a room.'

Bowman imagined what a life the boy must lead. By rights he should have been in the workhouse. There at least he would have been schooled. And yet he was doing well enough. He'd found a roof for his head at night, and even an apprenticeship to a trade. Bowman had a feeling that, his present circumstances resolved, Archie would do well. He resisted the urge to ruffle the lad's hair.

'This is Lily.' Bowman turned to see Graves had brought the barmaid over. She twisted her cloth in her hands nervously. 'It's alright, Lily,' Graves soothed. 'Just tell the inspector what you told me.'

'They was in here right enough. Seven of 'em there was, sat at that long table there.' She pointed at the long trestle nearest the fire. 'Drinking and swearing, like they was 'appy with themselves. Came in about four and left at the bell.'

'Was that unusual?' Bowman looked up at the girl from where he sat.

'Not so much. Though maybe during the week. Their normal night's a Friday, on account of 'em not openin' at the weekend.' Bowman allowed himself a wry smile. O'Sheehy's jibe at 'Scotland Yard hours' suddenly rang rather hollow. 'And there's normally eight o'them, too. They take up the whole table.'

'Would you know them if you saw them?'

'O'course! Spent all me time trying to keep their hands off me, didn't I?'

'And you are certain there were seven of them?'

Bowman's voice had taken on a tone Graves recognised. He was on to something, he knew.

'I'm not so daft as I can't count. If I say there was seven of 'em, then seven there was.' Lily turned with a harrumph and strutted back to the bar and her business, clearly trying her best to look as insulted as possible. Not so insulted though, noticed Bowman, that she didn't find the time to give Sergeant Graves another look as she passed. The sergeant took his seat at the table, dismissing Bowman's look with a wave of his hand. The inspector had Boothby's ledger open at the table now, leafing through its pages with a look of concentration on his face.

'The men we spoke to all said Boothby had been here with them last night,' he muttered, almost to himself.

'Who's to say he wasn't?' Graves was trying to follow Bowman's train of thought.

'Lily, for one.' Smoothing the pages open with a hand, Bowman directed Graves' attention to a table of numbers and names, all written in an angular, spidery hand.

'Here's a list of stalls, from one to a hundred and eight,' he explained. 'Together with an inventory of the names attached to them. Sergeant Graves, which of the men did you interview in the course of your duties earlier?'

Graves had drawn a notebook from his pocket. 'One man at number thirty-five, one at thirty-six and two at thirty-seven.'

Bowman rattled off their names from the ledger, 'Prentice, Adams, Wallace and Samuelson.'

'They all said they were here last night,' Graves confirmed, leaning over the ledger to read further. 'Johns and Carter at thirty-eight had both gone home to their wives, Hudson at thirty-nine met his sweetheart at Covent Garden.'

Bowman nodded. 'I spoke to O'Sheehy and his lad at thirty-three and Griffiths at thirty-two. All three said they were here last night. To get fettled after a day's graft.'

'Then there's our seven,' Graves concluded.

Bowman turned to his companion, his eyes alive with the thrill of the moment. 'Then where was Boothby when Hibbert died?' Bowman was about to slam the ledger shut, but something in its pages had evidently caught Graves' attention.

'Wait, sir, see here.' He was pointing to the rows next to each numbered stall. Tracing up with his finger, he could see each entry in the row denoted the rent each trader had paid to Boothby on each successive week.

'What of it, Graves? It's as you would expect, a list of the rents paid for the market stalls.'

'I'm not looking at what has been written, sir, I'm looking at how it's been written.'

Bowman angled the ledger to the window, the better to see what was written there. In the morning light, it was clear what Graves had meant. Each entry had been written in the same ink until November the twenty third. A different ink had been employed from then on. That was nothing unusual in itself, thought Bowman, but placing the book in the light had brought Graves' point into sharp relief. The new ink had started earlier along Hibbert's row, from September of the last year.

'What do you think that means, sir?' Graves' eyes were

wide in thought.

'One of two things, Graves. Either Boothby used a different ink for Hibbert, and only Hibbert, for two months. Or, he went back later and filled in blank entries so as not to appear suspicious.'

Graves was confused. 'Why would there be blank spaces? Surely Hibbert paid his rent each week?'

'I can't imagine Boothby giving him anything but short shrift if he didn't.' Bowman was suddenly all action. 'Come on Graves,' he barked, snatching his hat from the table. 'We need to get that market open.'

'But you gave the order that the gates should be shut. I told Boothby myself.' Graves couldn't help but be incredulous.

Bowman turned. 'They're traders, Graves. So let them trade!' The inspector left the table with a flurry, leaving Sergeant Graves to gulp down the last of his pint and Archie Walton to finish his eels.

'The man's not worth the bother,' proclaimed Arthur Boothby, his flat northern vowels all the broader in his passion. 'The market's better off without him.'

'He was murdered, Mr Boothby,' Bowman sounded an exasperated note. 'And violently at that.' He stood opposite the market manager in his office high above the trading floor. Below them, the public had at last been allowed to enter and they flooded in as if a dam had burst. They spilled into every corner with a bustling, eager activity. The inspector had surprised Sergeant Graves with his sudden insistence that the market be opened, but

Bowman was formulating a plan. In order for it to work, each butcher would have to sell his wares today in order that another delivery would be made that night. He was pleased to see from his vantage that trading was brisk. To his left, a parade of sheep was fetching a good price at auction. To his right, O'Sheehy was haggling with his customer over a consignment of beef.

'For The Savoy, no less,' remarked Boothby, joining Bowman at the window. 'They do their business with us and us only. They're renowned for their beef as you may know, inspector.' Boothby knew the menu at The Savoy to be well out of reach of a detective's salary. 'Well, that beef comes from our market. And the commission doesn't harm, neither,' he winked. 'Did you make much progress on the floor?'

'I did,' Bowman lied. He was never one to show his hand, especially if he was lacking in the crucial cards. 'Mr Boothby, could you assure me you were at The Bishop's Finger last night?'

'I can that. I went for a drink with some of the men. I go back years with O'Sheehy and his boy. Aye, and some others, too. We make a point of drinking together once in a while.' He narrowed his eyes. 'Is that a crime, inspector?'

Bowman took the time to look around the office. A large, ostentatious desk was set against a far wall, laden with piles and sheaves of paper. A battered, leather chair stood behind, its upholstery torn and tattered. This was the only furniture save a simple wooden chair for visitors and three sets of shelves that groaned under the weight of boxes and files stuffed to bursting with yet more paper. Windows at either side gave out to the market. As Boothby stood at the centre of the room, his eyes darting occasionally to the traders as they went about their business below, he looked to Bowman like nothing less than a spider at the centre of its web. Bowman was sure the man was alive to every quiver on every thread, perhaps with an intent just as deadly. He slammed the ledger down on the table by way of a response. Two or three papers fluttered to the floor. Boothby's eyebrows twitched in agitation.

'You are thorough in your bookkeeping, Mr Boothby?' Bowman looked directly at the man, watching for any signs of hesitation.

'That I am, inspector,' Boothby sighed. He spoke slowly and deliberately, as if for the benefit of an elderly relative. 'There's men down there that rely upon it.'

'You collect the rent each week?'

'I do.'

Bowman nodded, leafing through the pages of the ledger until he reached the list of names he had noticed in The Bishop's Finger. 'What does this table represent, Mr Boothby?' he asked, simply.

Boothby snorted. Could a Scotland Yarder be so devoid of nous? 'That is the table of payments, inspector. You'll see from there that every man must pay on a Friday.'

'And they are all up to date?'

'They are.' Boothby had folded his arms across his not insubstantial chest.

'Could you tell me why Solomon Hibbert ceased paying his rent in September of last year, yet you allowed him to

34

continue at your market?'

The silence was palpable. Bowman felt he could reach out into the room and touch it. Arthur Boothby cleared his throat. Bowman knew he was buying time.

'Well, inspector, I see you have the better of me.'

'Hibbert's row in the table was originally blank from September twenty first,' Bowman continued. 'Yet you went back and filled in those spaces with another ink, which you started using in November.' Boothby's eyes were darting about him. He had the demeanour of a trapped man. 'Why?' Boothby was tight-lipped. The inspector ploughed on. 'He had not paid his rent in nine weeks, Mr Boothby. In fact, I would venture that he had not paid his rent from that day to this. How could you countenance such a thing?'

Boothby stood swaying slowly on his feet. With a slow, deliberate movement, he loped towards his chair and flung his weight upon it. 'I'm a charitable man, Inspector Bowman. You're right about the rent. Hibbert hadn't paid me since September. I altered the ledger to save myself. If the other traders twigged he'd been getting his stall gratis, they'd be all over me like flies at a window. Truth be told, I was on the point of throwing him out. Enough is enough, Inspector Bowman, and Hibbert had been tweaking me by the nose for too long. He was a scoundrel and a drunk, and I let him take advantage of my better nature.' Boothby tried his best to affect a pious air. 'I knew he was poor. He'd drunk his money away and scarcely had enough to pay his boy.' Bowman knew he was lying. Mrs Hibbert's dress and collection of trinkets, let alone the box of money beneath her hearth, spoke of a wealthier man than Boothby was painting. 'I dare say he owed money elsewhere too, and it was that that got him fettled.'

The sudden tilt in Bowman's head was almost imperceptible. 'Fettled?' he echoed back, raising an eyebrow.

Boothby laughed. 'Fixed, inspector. Sorted. It's a hang-up from the old country. I've lived in London almost thirty years, yet still I'm drawn to the northern way of things. Hibbert was fettled; sorted good and proper.'

'The men I interviewed this morning spoke of having a drink to fettle them after a day at the market.'

Boothby's eyes glittered in defiance. 'So?'

'Why would they say such a thing, unless they had been schooled to say so?'

There was a pause as Boothby considered what next to do. 'I am a busy man, inspector,' he began, rising to his feet. 'As I expect are you. If you are done with your questions, I had rather get to work. There is, after all, a market to run.' Boothby gestured to the crowds out the window.

'Of course.' Bowman placed his hat back on his head and straightened his coat about him. It was clear he'd get no more from Boothby. As he descended the steps from the manager's office, he mulled their conversation over in his mind. Boothby was hiding something, that much was certain. Why did Hibbert refuse to pay his rent though he had money enough? How to explain where his money had come from? Frustratingly, his short interview with Arthur

Boothby had furnished him more questions than answers.

The temperature had plummeted. Much to Graves' surprise, Inspector Bowman had called a halt to the investigation immediately following his interview with Boothby.

'There is nothing further to be done, Graves,' Bowman knocked sawdust of his hat as they walked back to Farringdon Street station. 'At least not until tonight.' Even here on the platform, the ripe smell of livestock hung in the air. Bowman knew the line was shared with Smithfield Market, used as a boarding point for newly purchased cattle on their way to the slaughterhouses and abattoirs around London. 'Go home for now, Graves.' The inspector had to raise his voice against the squeal of an oncoming Metropolitan Railway train. Steam and dust filled the platform as it hissed to a halt before them. They took their seats.

'For now, sir?' Graves wiped soot from his eyes.

'Yes, Graves. We've got a long night ahead.'

'How so, sir?'

They felt the motion of the train as it pulled away from the platform and into the labyrinth of tunnels that would take it, ultimately, to Paddington.

'It's clear Hibbert had a hold over Boothby somehow. How else could he have withheld his rent and not been ejected from the market? Yet Boothby went to some lengths to cover up the fact.'

'By altering the records in the ledger.' Graves was

nodding, slowly.

'What doesn't he want us to know, Graves? And just where was Hibbert's money coming from?'

'I suppose with no rent to pay, he was a sight better off than the other traders.'

Bowman smoothed his wide moustache with a finger and thumb, his frown cutting deep on his forehead. 'There's more to it than that, Graves. There was more in that tin than I could earn in a six month. Get yourself home, brush the sawdust from your clothes and get some sleep. It might be a long night.'

The sky above them was clear. Stars pricked the sky. A full moon lit the way as Bowman and Graves moved carefully through Middle Street into Cloth Fair. They had both made something of an effort by way of disguise. Sergeant Graves wore a shabby cap and overcoat with a greasy apron tied around his waist. Inspector Bowman peered out from under a shapeless, felt hat. His lean figure was swamped in a pair of overalls and a tradesman's coat. He was confident that, provided they kept out of the way of Boothby and the other men they had spoken to, they would not be recognised. The bustle would be such that they could observe unnoticed. At least, that was the hope.

Already they could hear the cries of the deliverymen and the traders at the market. The moaning of cattle mixed with the occasional bleat from the lambs as livestock was corralled into pens within the huge structure before them. The Grand Avenue was crowded with men laden with cuts of meat, livestock being herded to their enclosures and marshals and foremen pointing the way. Through it all, Bowman could see Arthur Boothby. He was standing on an upturned crate, directing proceedings with a cane. Ticking off items in his ledger as they arrived, he was clearly in his element. Pages were drawn from the leather pouch at his side and handed to traders and deliverymen for signing. Now and then, his flat northern vowels would sing out with a command or a jest to be answered with a laugh, a curse or an oath from one or other of the traders around him.

'What are we looking for, sir?' The two men had stepped back into a doorway across the road.

'Anything out of the ordinary, Graves.' Bowman had pulled his hat further down his head and turned up the collar on his coat, the better to hide his face. 'If we get separated, we'll meet at St. Sepulchre's.' Graves nodded in understanding. Keeping to what shadows there were, the two detectives stepped across the road behind a passing cart. Three sheep stared balefully out at them as it rattled past. Comically, Graves raised a finger to his lips to bid them quiet. He smiled at Bowman, impressed at his own joke. The pair slunk close to the edge of the great entrance, timing their movements with when there was the most activity around them. Stepping carefully through the dung and straw, they made their way off the Grand Avenue and into the market proper.

'You there!' A voice rang out amongst the hubbub, coarse and commanding. 'Hey!' The two men paused. To ignore such a shout would be to arouse suspicion. Bowman adopted an affected nonchalance as Graves turned to face a thickset man with half a pig slung over his shoulder.

'Make yerself useful,' he rasped. 'And get this pig to number thirty-eight.'

Graves seemed to relish the opportunity. Stepping forward eagerly, he took the weight of the carcass and shrugged it over his shoulder. 'Then get yerself back to the cart,' continued the man, oblivious. 'There's more to be carried and we're short on time.' He cleared his throat. Spitting phlegm to the floor, he wiped his mouth with a sleeve, jammed a soggy cigarette between his teeth and loped back towards the entrance and his cart.

Graves turned to Bowman so the pig and he were face to face. 'Looks like I've got the perfect cover, sir.'

'Very good, Graves,' Bowman swallowed hard to quell his disgust. 'You're a natural.'

'Hang about, sir,' Graves' voice had fallen to a whisper and he gave a nod to a corner across the hall, 'What's going on over there?'

Bowman turned to where Graves had gestured. Away from the crowd, a single cart stood by the farthest wall. Looking about him, Bowman could see the majority of traders were avoiding it. Some affected sideways glances or shook their heads as they saw it. Others nodded and shrugged or rolled their eyes to their colleagues. The cart was clearly the subject of some discussion, but no one seemed keen to approach it. No one, except the seven men who presently rounded a corner, rubbing their hands with anticipation. They were led by a portly man with a shock of ginger hair and a pipe.

'O'Sheehy,' breathed Bowman. 'And his lad. That man

behind them is Griffiths. I spoke to him this morning.'

'As did I the other four.' Graves had manoeuvred himself so as to be hidden behind the pig at his shoulder.

'What are they doing at that cart, Graves? And why is it being given such a wide berth by the others?'

'Only one way to find out, sir.' Before the inspector could object, Graves had stepped out into the throng, using the pig as a shield as he skirted round the hall to the farthest corner. Glancing to the men once more, Bowman could see them being led to the back of the cart by the driver. He pulled aside a blood-stained sheet to reveal a pile of meat. The men nodded their heads with enthusiasm and shook the man by the hand before each taking a substantial joint of meat and slinging it over their shoulders. Bowman watched aghast as Graves neared the cart. As the men staggered back to their stalls with their load, he saw his companion discard his pig in a pile of hessian sacks. Keeping low, Graves rounded the cart. Choosing his moment as the driver mounted the cab, the young detective sergeant ran for the trailer and flung himself under the bloodied sheet. Bowman fought back the urge to shout an objection. With a crack of his whip and a whistle, the driver bade his horse move on. Bowman shrunk back into the shadows as the cart gained speed. It kicked up dirt and dung as it passed, the traders regarding it suspiciously as it rattled away. Bowman raised his eyes to the ceiling and hissed through gritted teeth.

'Graves...'

Detective Sergeant Anthony Graves lay low. He had felt

every bump and rut in the road as he was carried along the narrow streets around Smithfield. Only once had he feared discovery. The cart had slowed as they left the market and Graves heard Boothby's distinctive vowels but a few feet away.

'Drive safe now, Absolom. I take it you've left us some nice, choice cuts this morning?'

Graves heard a chuckle from the driver and then the whip cracked again. With a jerk, they left the market at speed, careening round the corner onto West Smithfield. Graves tried to keep a track of their direction. Once or twice he peered through a hole in the sheet, but beyond Clerkenwell Road he had lost his bearings. Some forty minutes passed. Every muscle in his body complained at being held in such a cramped condition on such a cold night. Just as he feared he would freeze, Graves felt the cart slow. They were passing over rougher ground now, and Graves hazarded they had left the main road. Daring to peek from beneath the sheet, he saw that they were now in open country. At the speed they had travelled, Graves guessed a distance of some eight to ten miles had been traversed. In which direction, he knew not. They passed a forbidding farmhouse and pulled up beside an old outbuilding at which the driver jumped from his seat. From his cramped location, Graves watched as the man disappeared inside. A lamp was lit at a window. The sergeant waited a few minutes then slowly pulled the sheet back. Crouching low, he dropped from the trailer and ran to a nearside wall, being sure to keep his body flat against the brickwork. He took the time to get his bearings. The outbuilding was of a single storey and backed onto a rough yard surrounded on three sides by a wall. Long wooden poles were slung along its length, each studded at intervals with chains. A dozen hulking shapes loomed from the darkness. Graves moved a step nearer, the better to peer into the gloom. As a cloud passed the moon, the shapes revealed themselves. They were horses. Graves knew they had seen him, but none seemed to have the strength to react. Approaching carefully, he saw that they were old and grizzled. One had protruding ribs and running sores upon its back, another had legs so thin Graves feared they would snap at any moment. Looking about him he saw one on the floor. The unfortunate creature was lying prone in the dirt, its sides rising and falling in time to a hideous rattle. Clearly, the beasts were near death. Graves uttered a soothing word or two under his breath then mad his way to the end of the yard. There, in an unceremonious heap by the door of a smaller building, was a pile of bones. Shoulder blades protruded from the mire, great leg bones lay in haphazard heaps. A horse's skull lay on top of a pile, its sightless sockets staring blankly into the night. Graves shuddered at the sight.

Putting his shoulder to the door, he eased into the shed behind the yard to be greeted by a stench like nothing he had ever known. It stung his eyes and caught in his throat. Before him in the gloom, he could just make out a great, steaming vat. A viscous liquid bubbled and popped within. To his right he saw a long butcher's block piled high with rough cuts of meat. Graves had seen enough. It was one thing if O'Sheehy and his ilk had been fraudulently selling horse meat at Smithfield Market. That the meat had its source at such a wretched and despicable charnel house was another matter entirely. A hand held over his face to stifle the smell, Graves made his way from the shed and into the yard once more. He regarded the horses sadly, standing for a moment in silence with them. Then, his face a mask of resolve, he took a breath to steel himself.

Making suddenly for the perimeter, he bounded onto the cart at the entrance, snapped at the reins and steered it with a clatter back to the main road. In time, he hoped, he would see some landmark to guide him back to London. As he rattled through the gate, Graves noticed a hand-painted sign fixed to the fence at a crazy angle. Pushing the horse to give him yet more speed, he nonetheless had time to read the words printed on it as he passed; HARRY ABSOLOM, KNACKER'S YARD.

St. Sepulchre's stood like a sentinel in the night. A haven of divinity in an area given to carnal fulfillment, it had withstood fire and plague and civil war. Inspector Bowman stood regarding the altar, lifting his eyes to the crucifix above. The figure of Christ was a fragile thing. How could such a slight figure withstand such pain, he wondered. How could anyone bear such pain? Bowman fought the inclination to kneel. He would not bend or he would break. For a moment she was with him, her hand on his shoulder, her head inclined to his. She met his gaze and smoothed the furrow at his brow. And with a kiss, she was gone. Bowman felt alone. Turning about, he saw Sergeant Graves walking briskly through the transept door, his footsteps echoing up to the vaulted ceiling.

'That was reckless, Graves,' Bowman admonished him as he approached.

'Desperate times called for desperate measures, sir.'

'That's as may be, sergeant,' Bowman snapped. 'But I had rather you consult me first before embarking on such adventures.'

'Some adventure,' Graves sighed.

'What did you find?' Bowman asked.

'Hell, inspector.' Graves had lost his customary smile. 'I found Hell.'

The Empire might well span half the globe, mused Arthur Boothby as he stood at the top of the steps leading to his office, but he could give it a run for its money. Looking below him, he felt a sense of pride at his dominion. Counters groaned with meat in anticipation of the day's trade, butchers stood poised for the sale, cuts of every size hung from every wall. To his right, livestock awaited their fate, their nostrils steaming in anticipation. Shepherds and farmers gathered in knots to talk. And, over it all, Arthur Boothby held sway. Walking down the steps to the main gates, Boothby let his eyes wander from stall to stall. Few traders met his eye, some even looked away as he passed. No matter. If they wanted a stall at Smithfield they'd have to lump him. He chuckled to himself, his mean mouth stretching into something resembling a smile. The Scotland Yarders had disappeared as fast as they had come. Boothby fancied the Bowman fellow had given it up as a bad job. With Hibbert out the way, all was clear.

In a little less than ten years, Boothby mused, he would leave the market and buy a smallholding near the sea back in the old country. Morecambe Bay had always been a favourite, and he fancied he might live out his final days in comfort, staring at the sea from his modest house. Now he must be certain that O'Sheehy and his gang would be true to their word. Perhaps Hibbert might prove an example to them. Pulling a chain of keys from his pocket, Boothby put a hand to the gates to steady himself. It was going to be a busy day.

'Let's leave those shut, shall we?' Feeling a hand at his shoulder, Boothby turned to find himself face to face with Sergeant Graves. 'Inspector Bowman wants a word.' The sergeant stepped aside to reveal the inspector standing some way off. Beside him stood O'Sheehy and his lad, Griffiths, Prentice, Adams, Wallace and Samuelson.

'The market's sealed, Boothby. No one's coming or going.' Bowman had his hands in his pockets, his coat pulled tight around him.

'The game's up, Arthur.' O'Sheehy's Irish drawl was thick with defeat. The seven men behind the inspector looked downcast, their shoulders slumped in dejection.

'They've as good as confessed, Boothby,' Bowman called.

Boothby sensed he was trapped. With his back to the gates he had nowhere to run. 'Confessed to what?' he hissed.

Bowman took a step forward, the lamps on the wall behind him lengthening his shadow across the floor. 'To being accessories to the murder of Solomon Hibbert.'

Looking about him, Boothby could see a crowd was gathering. Traders were leaving their stalls to watch the proceedings. 'Then take them away and lock 'em up!'

Graves was smiling at him now. 'He said accessories to murder. There's another who took the lead.'

Boothby stared wildly about him. 'Then catch him! String him up!'

'They might yet do that, Arthur.' O'Sheehy was holding up a conciliatory hand. 'Give it up, man.'

Boothby appealed to the detectives. 'But I was at The Bishop's Finger all that night. The men'll tell you that.' At the mention of the public house, Bowman stood aside to admit another. A young woman took his place, blinking into the cold, morning air. The crowd exchanged nudges. Graves' eyes grew wide. Swathed in a coat and scarf, Lily looked all the more voluptuous. By rights she should be warm in her bed, she thought, but this inspector chap was quite the persistent sort.

'Lily,' Bowman was saying, 'do you know these men?'

Lily looked around at the ramshackle group. 'Know 'em? I spend half me time tryin' to avoid 'em.' The spectators laughed at this. Lily, enjoying her audience, gifted them a smile.

'Could you tell me,' Bowman continued, 'which of these men were at The Bishop's Finger the night before last?'

Lily looked around and raised an arm to point at each man in the group. As her accusing finger damned them in turn, they each looked to the ground.

Bowman raised an eyebrow in mock enquiry. 'But not

Mr Boothby?'

Lily shook her head, 'No, not him. Not that night.'

Boothby stood stock-still. 'Your story was a lie, was it not, Mr Boothby?' Bowman was circling him now. 'Cooked up to cover your absence. It was unfortunate that none of your gang had the wit to find their own words.'

'To what end?' Boothby demanded, his arms wide. 'Why would I want Hibbert dead?'

Bowman turned his head to his companion. 'Graves?'

'I took a little ride this morning, Mr Boothby. Or rather, I was taken.'

'What is this?' Boothby jeered.

'The inspector and I were party to some unusual activity last night,' Graves continued, 'Right here at Smithfield Market. While your traders took their deliveries in the small hours of the morning, we found a Mr Harry Absolom plying his trade.' Boothby blanched at the name. 'I jumped his cart. As you bid him have a safe journey, I lay under a sheet just four feet from you.' Graves smiled again. Boothby's eyes darted left and right, thinking through the repercussions of the sergeant's words.

'We know your deal with Absolom,' Bowman was face to face with Boothby now. 'And so did Hibbert. Didn't he, Mr Boothby?'

Boothby remained tight-lipped.

'Hibbert wasn't happy,' O'Sheehy interjected. 'We all knew that. The inspector tells me he stopped paying rent in protest, but that you covered it up so we wouldn't know.' Fists clenched before him, it was clear O'Sheehy was itching for a fight.

'He threatened to expose us!' roared Boothby, cornered. 'What would you have me do?'

'You paid him hush money,' O'Sheehy was flexing his hands. 'Our money.'

The traders around them had started to protest and jeer. 'We knew there was something crooked going on,' declared one. 'We wanted no part of it,' proclaimed another.

Bowman understood. 'Stanley Kelley!' he called. A young man stepped forward, his face a mask of defiance. Bowman clapped a hand upon his shoulder. 'This is Stanley Kelley. An upright man if ever there was one. And I should imagine there are many more such men here.' Shouts of agreement rang out.

'You have debased our trade.' Kelley's lip was quivering with emotion.

'It's only horse meat!' Boothby threw back his head and roared. 'It's good enough for the Frenchies.'

'Good enough for The Savoy, would you say?' Bowman's moustache twitched. 'That meat is culled under such conditions as to be unsafe. It is not fit for consumption. That alone would be enough to see you lose your licence.'

Voices rang out to punctuate the morning air, 'Take it off him!' called one.

'As low as he was,' continued Bowman, the crowd at his back, 'Hibbert would not see his trade perverted. But soon, you lost your patience. Concocting a story to protect yourself, you sent your men to The Bishop's Finger while you lay in wait. Alice Hibbert told me of your weekly meetings, after which her husband would return with fists full of notes.'

'Our money!' snorted O'Sheehy, his feet scuffing the ground.

'Two nights ago, Hibbert left for his meeting, but he was never to return.' The crowd was silent now. They may have shared no love for Hibbert, but none amongst them would have seen him harmed. 'You set about him, did you not?' Bowman looked around at the butcher's stalls. Each had the instruments of their trade hung from hooks. 'It is not hard to see where you might have found your weapons.'

'He put up a fight, for sure,' Boothby relented, his shoulders slumped.

'And then O'Sheehy and the others returned from the inn to help you carry him here.' Bowman was toe to toe with him again. 'Only you had the keys to the gate.' Bowman held out a hand. Boothby hesitated before handing over the keys. The inspector's hand closed around them. 'Your men stuck him on a hook,' he continued. 'As a warning to others to hold their tongue. It took four men to get him down, I dare say it would have taken double to get him up, slippery with blood as he was.'

There were murmurings amongst the crowd.

'He deserves to hang,' said Kelley, his eyes ablaze. 'They all do.'

Boothby looked about him, suddenly exposed. He would never go down at the hands of a baying mob. His eyes fell on O'Sheehy. The Irishman had broken ranks. Whatever he had told the inspector, it had been too much. Boothby felt his blood rising and the prospect of a comfortable retirement in Morecambe Bay slipping away. With a roar, he charged at the man, barrelling into him at speed. Caught off guard, O'Sheehy fell to the floor with a thud, his head cracking hard against the stone.

At a signal from Bowman, Graves took a whistle from his pocket and blew. There was an immediate stillness in the market. Even Boothby let his quarry go in surprise. O'Sheehy took the advantage of the moment to punch his assailant square in the jaw. Approaching footsteps could be heard from around the corner near the market entrance. They were running.

Bowman sprung to the gate, deftly turning the key in the lock to admit half a dozen constables in uniform and Detective Inspector Ignatius Hicks. As the constables ran to apprehend the gang under Graves' direction, Hicks approached Bowman with a swagger.

'Well done, Inspector Bowman,' he breathed. Bowman was careful to show no emotion. 'Of course, I would have had all this wrapped up if you'd called upon me sooner.'

'Indeed,' agreed Bowman, deadpan. 'But I did not think it wise to disturb you at your breakfast.'

As the constables rounded up their charges, Bowman turned to Stanley Kelley and met his eye. 'Mr Kelley,' he called across the concourse. 'Get this market open and you may proceed with your trade.' With that, he threw him the keys and turned away, the faintest of smiles playing upon his lips.

~

THE HACKNEY POISONING

MARCH, 1892

Sir Kingdom Fanshawe stood at the gates to Hackney Union Workhouse, resting his great frame upon his ornate cane. Fashioned from wood said to have been brought from the Amazon basin, he fancied it gave him an air of mystery and profound wisdom. His great Astrakhan coat brushed the road where he stood such that, within moments of stepping from his carriage, the hems were caked with dust and grime. A fancy waistcoat barely contained the great expanse of his stomach. The material was of a deep, luxurious red. His cravat was secured at his neck with a jewel in the form of a scarab beetle. Most remarkable of all, however, was his face. For one who had made his money through foreign investments, it seemed entirely appropriate that it resembled nothing less than a map. His veins were the rivulets and tributaries of a great river, his nose a promontory. His eyes were two deep, rheumy lakes, his pock-marked skin the pitted terrain of a scarred desert. A pair of dark beetle brows crowned the whole, like two great and unruly forests. A thatch of dark hair was swept back from the tundra of his forehead and crowned with a tall, silk top hat. All in all, Sir Kingdom liked to think, he cut quite the figure as he stood on Homerton High Street before the workhouse.

It had been a rainy night and the high walls reared from the filthy road towards grey, roiling clouds. Behind those walls, Sir Kingdom knew, there existed a world in opposition to his own. Where he knew luxury and comfort, those who lived in the dormitories that rose before him knew only poverty and hardship. Where he had the world at his feet, the walls before him contained world enough for those inside. Where he considered himself master of his own fate, those poor wretches were destined for one thing only; an early grave. The workhouse was home to some five hundred people, staff and inmates. It was a community of the poorest and most desperate in society. It provided security of sorts to those at the bottom of the heap. Those with nothing found themselves at its gates, to find they still had nothing but had to work for it. A roof and strict discipline were all the workhouse had to offer. Men were put to work in the breaking yards or in the cobbler's workshops. Women toiled at the laundry or in the kitchens. It had often struck Sir Kingdom as a rum thing that the inmates' toil should be to provide for the inmates themselves. In his capacity as the prime benefactor, he had access to the register of inmates. He knew those walls contained amongst their number a good many cabinetmakers, bricklayers, glassblowers and needlewomen. Surely, they would be better put to work for some other, greater, good? Principally, Sir Kingdom's good. He drew deep on his cigar as he considered the many hundreds of pounds he had gifted the workhouse. He saw now, as the smoke encircled his head, that it had all been wasted. He had seen no return in the last three years. In that time, conditions at the workhouse had deteriorated. A new, more lax regime had resulted in a breakdown of discipline. Fights amongst the inmates were commonplace, often resulting in injury or death. Respect for the staff had disappeared and they were often the recipients of verbal or physical abuse. As a result, the workhouse had lost five of its ten staff and were having trouble recruiting their replacements. Now, it only attracted those to its gates who were of a more belligerent personality. A black market in cigarettes and opium had flourished behind those walls, and brawls between rival factions were commonplace. Meal times were often abandoned as they descended into chaos and the factories and yards were brought to a standstill. Hackney's reputation had travelled far and wide. Those in Sir Kingdom's circle were beginning to question the wisdom of his investment in the workhouse. This was leading to a lack of confidence in his whole portfolio. One by one, his clients were deserting him. To put it simply, Hackney Union Workhouse was bad for his business.

Sir Kingdom trod the stump of his cigar into the ground and made his way to the great iron gates that marked the entrance. The master of the workhouse, a dandy of a man in green frock coat and bejewelled waistcoat, was already at the gate with his keys, a sycophantic smile upon his face. A tidy, officious-looking moustache bristled on his top lip.

'Sir Kingdom,' Ferdinand Barrett leered as he bent at the lock, 'It is a pleasure to see you again. I trust you are well?' He adjusted his silk cravat at his throat as he spoke. Sir Kingdom noted it did not match the colour of his waistcoat.

The knight harrumphed as the gate swung open to admit him.

'I am so sorry I am late,' Barrett continued. 'There was a little trouble in the breaking yard.' Sir Kingdom nodded, curtly. He fancied he had heard the commotion over the wall as he had waited on the road. 'Rest assured that matters have been brought to a satisfactory conclusion.' Sir Kingdom noticed the master was rubbing a bruise on his jaw as he spoke.

'Very good, Barrett,' Sir Kingdom rumbled. 'I trust it will not delay dinner? I have many calls upon my time.' He pulled an ornate fob watch from his waistcoat, tapped the dial and tutted loudly.

'No, indeed,' breathed Barrett as he led his companion across the yard to the master's quarters. 'The food will be ready to serve in just a few minutes and the staff are already assembled.'

Sir Kingdom rolled his eyes to the grey heavens above. These monthly dinners were nothing but a chore and he would be glad to be shot of them. They had been instigated at the previous master's insistence and, in truth, Sir Kingdom had enjoyed his company. He had thrilled to Sir Kingdom's tales of his travels and the subsequent investments that had brought him his wealth; the spice trade in India, the cotton fields of China, the vineyards of France. In short, he had felt flattered by the attention and happy to increase his largesse accordingly. It had been a prestige investment, given only so that Sir Kingdom's reputation might benefit. And so it did. He was praised for his philanthropy. He carried his reputation with him in his demeanour; his back never anything less than ramrod straight, his nose never held anything less than high into the air.

Barrett led him through the rear door to his apartments. As Sir Kingdom stepped over the threshold, he fancied he heard a cat-call from across the yard behind him. Turning, he saw several men leaning out of a high window in the building opposite, their hands outstretched to deliver the most obscene gestures. They broke into laughter as they saw Sir Kingdom notice them.

'Awright, mate?' leered one through a mouth full of haphazard teeth. 'Come to 'elp in the kitchens, 'ave we?'

Barrett shut the door, an obsequious look upon his face. 'I can only apologise, Sir Kingdom,' he fawned. 'Some of the men are a little - ' he searched for the word, 'Excitable.'

The two men made their way up a wide wooden staircase into the master's parlour. There sat the staff, awaiting dinner. A stained, cotton cloth covered the dining table. The cutlery was of a tarnished steel that had seen better days and the glass was far from cut crystal. Frankly, thought Sir Kingdom Fanshawe as Barrett relieved him of his hat and coat, this was not what he was used to.

As he squeezed into his usual carver chair at the head of the table, the fat knight looked around him. Three men and a woman blinked back. The workhouse matron, Florence Habgood, looked like she had barely eaten anything in her life. Dark rings encircled her eyes and Sir Kingdom noticed she was losing her hair as she bobbed her head in greeting. Next to her sat Robert Coldman, the labour superintendent. He raised his glass as he met Sir Kingdom's eyes, his mean lips breaking into something approaching a smile. Then came William Mooney, the ward superintendent. A fidgety young man with a lopsided face, he looked away as Sir Kingdom's gaze swept the table. Almost directly opposite, sat Ambrose the caretaker. An ancient scarecrow of a man, he sat bent at the table, his beady eyes and bony hands restless in anticipation of his meal. As Ferdinand Barrett took his place to his left hand side, Sir Kingdom Fanshawe looked balefully around the table and concluded it was populated by the least interesting company he could possibly imagine.

The meal was inadequate in both quality and quantity. A bland bird had been boiled a good half hour longer than was necessary. The vegetables were hard and unforgiving, the sauce a thin brown soup. Even the wine could not lift Sir Kingdom's spirits. Dinner was taken in almost complete silence. As each course was brought to the table by the matron from the kitchen below, those around him raised their eyes to the knight in hopeful expectation of a kind word or look concerning the food. None was forthcoming.

Over pudding, a steamed sponge of questionable heritage, Barrett finally found his voice. 'I am sure, Sir Kingdom,' he began through a mouthful of dried fruit, 'that you will be most impressed with the improvements to the privy.' Sir Kingdom paused with his food half way to his lip, his appetite suddenly diminished. 'We have now erected a wall to keep it from the gaze of the other inmates.'

William Mooney nodded, thoughtfully. 'This was as a direct result of requests from some of the women,' he added. 'We are often minded to remember that we are here to serve them.'

Sir Kingdom's brows darkened. He resented the remark. These people were not to be served. They were, if possible, to be profited from.

To his left, Barrett was opening a box of cut cigars. He had learnt that the easiest way to impress the knight was to offer him a cigar after a meal. In truth, Sir Kingdom had always found Barrett's choice of smoke rather inferior. The leaf was too try, the tobacco too woody. Taking a cigar from the box, Sir Kingdom absently cut the end and held it to a candle on the table. Puffing it to life, he leaned back on his chair and cleared his throat. 'Have you instigated the programme of employment I suggested when last we met?' Barrett's blank look told him he had not. 'There is a body of able men here,' Sir Kingdom continued through billows of smoke, 'who are capable of service to the outside world. Things may be mended, roads may be maintained, shoes may be fixed. And all for a price.' His eyes gleamed.

'We do not feel,' stuttered the master, 'that such things are within the purview of the workhouse.'

'You are weak, sir!' Sir Kingdom banged his fist against the table. 'Weak!' The matron jumped in surprise at the noise and held her hand to her mouth.

'I have seen my investments squandered on these ridiculous, hare-brained schemes.' Sir Kingdom was on his feet now. 'A wall to hide the privy, indeed.' He dabbed at his mouth with a soiled napkin. 'You forget sir, that these people know nothing better. They are used to squatting in the street!' He turned to the matron. 'With apologies, madam.' Florence Habgood did her best to give a demure nod. Sir Kingdom turned his attention back to the workhouse master. 'Why should my money be spent on a wall?'

The caretaker raised a bony finger. 'We used brick from the breaking yard, sir,' he offered.

'I care nothing for the breaking yard.' Sir Kingdom had walked from the table to the coat stand by the front door. 'I care nothing for the inmates,' he was shrugging on his heavy coat as he seethed. 'And I care nothing for this workhouse.'

'What is your meaning, sir?' blustered Barrett from his seat.

'I mean to withdraw my benevolence, sir.' There were audible gasps from around the table. 'This place is bringing me nothing but misery. Your ill-repute has spread as surely as if it were one of the diseases in your infirmary.' The matron's mouth hung open. 'My clients are deserting me, hearing of my association with this failing workhouse.'

Barrett was on his feet at once, his hands held wide. 'But, Sir Kingdom, without your money,' he stammered, 'We will struggle to stay open.'

'Seems to me you're struggling already.' Sir Kingdom jammed his top hat on his head and bent to retrieve his cane.

'Will you go public with your decision?' asked Coldman, agog. 'The news will destroy us.'

'None knows but my wife, as she knows all of my affairs. Tomorrow, I shall inform the Board of Guardians. From then on, the world shall know.' He swung round to face Barrett. 'I cannot continue to prop you up, Barrett,' he thundered. 'You must find yourself another benefactor.'

With that, Sir Kingdom Fanshawe swept from the room leaving a stunned audience in his wake. Ferdinand Barrett stood blinking at the table, his spoon still held in his hand. 'Mr Coldman,' he began, slowly. 'I think preparations should be made.'

'Preparations for what, sir?' asked Robert Coldman as he stood in his place.

Barrett swallowed as he looked around the table. Those seated next to him depended on the workhouse for their income. Without it, they too would be cast upon the streets. He could see from their faces that the truth was presenting itself to them. Without Sir Kingdom Fanshawe and his money, they didn't stand a chance. Barrett turned to Coldman, his lower lip quivering. 'Unemployment,' he said simply, and he sunk back into his chair.

Sir Kingdom Fanshawe felt a weight had been lifted from his shoulders. His only regret was that he had waited until the end of the meal before delivering his news. Had he come straight to the point earlier, he would have been spared one of the most forgettable dinners he had ever had the displeasure of eating. As his smart carriage whisked him south through the streets of Finsbury Park and Holloway, he felt glad to be shot of the place. The workhouse had proven to be a millstone around his neck. He would communicate his intention to the Board of Guardians first thing in the morning and soon, the greater world would know of it. Then he would tell his clients that he had had the wisdom to know a bad investment when he saw it. He had no doubt his business would then improve. He had made a great deal of money in the past, both as a banker and a broker, and had once handled a great many investments for a great many people. Perhaps he would again. Once word got round that he was shot of the workhouse, he was confident that his standing in financial circles would return. Happy at his afternoon's work, he puffed at the stump of his cigar as he eased himself back into his seat. The smoke left a bitter taste but still it was sufficient. Looking through the window he could see the sun breaking through the clouds. In brighter weather, London looked tolerable. Even the dingy streets of Camden looked more presentable in the sun. Not so presentable, however, mused Sir Kingdom Fanshawe, that he should ever want to be seen walking along them.

At last they were passing into more genteel streets and Sir Kingdom felt himself relax. Even Marylebone had a welcoming look about it. Its crowded streets and thoroughfares were at least wide and accommodating, and the buildings that lined the streets both grander and cleaner than any he had seen on his journey. The driver slowed as they approached Mayfair and Sir Kingdom let his eyes feast on familiar sights; pretty mews houses jostling for space around formal, well-planted squares and public gardens. Hyde Park spread out in front of him, and he could just make out the sun glinting off the waters of the Serpentine. Even in the cool March air, there were some brave enough to sit on the benches and read their newspapers. An elderly lady fed the pigeons with bread from her apron. A gaggle of children were led through the park by an efficient looking governess dressed in a wide crinoline dress and a neat bonnet. Sir Kingdom stretched in his seat. A tall man, he found carriage journeys to be generally uncomfortable. He rubbed his stiff neck with his hand and extended his leg to relieve the cramp in his foot.

He had chosen his house for one reason; its proximity to White's Gentlemen's Club. Sir Kingdom was of an age to remember the Duke of Wellington himself drinking there and hoped one day to be awarded the honour of having the very same table reserved for his use. It stood in the famous bow window on the ground floor and afforded the privilege of being both able to see those who entered and being seen by them. He felt his heart quicken as the carriage came to a stop outside the building's Palladian facade. The white Portland stone seemed to sparkle in the sun, and Sir Kingdom felt enthused at the prospect of an afternoon around the billiards table and an evening at the bar. Here at least, he thought, he would get a grouse cooked properly.

He stepped gingerly from the carriage and threw the stub of his cigar to the road. Smoothing his coat about him, he pulled himself up to his full height and prepared to enter the door of the only establishment in Britain he felt suited to a man of his position.

White's was considered the most exclusive gentlemen's club in the country. Possibly, Sir Kingdom liked to think, in the world. He climbed the few steps to the grand front door and beat against the knocker with his cane. In a few moments it was opened by a uniformed doorman. He nodded by way of a greeting and almost stood to attention as Sir Kingdom entered. Stopping only to give the man his hat and coat, Sir Kingdom passed immediately into the club's grand lounge, a lavish, high-ceilinged room with ornate furniture and a fine collection of country scenes in oil upon the walls. It was here that, at a little after half-past two, Sir Kingdom Fanshawe, Knight Commander of the British Empire, decorated for his service at Kanpur, arched his back with pain, frothed at the mouth, fell to the floor and died.

Number Twenty Four Park Lane stood on a quiet corner with Pitt's Head Mews, a network of narrow streets that led back from the east side of Hyde Park. It was an elegant, four-storey townhouse quite befitting its resident.

If any passing it had cared to look, they would have seen two men being greeted at the door by a footman. The taller of the men had a forlorn look about him, his hooded eyes telling of an intimacy with the cares of the world. The wider of them had a great beard and puffed almost compulsively on a long-stemmed pipe.

'I am Detective Inspector Bowman of Scotland Yard,' the leaner man said, quietly. 'And this is Inspector Hicks.'

The doorman turned to face the large, bearded man with

the pipe in his hand. As a concession to decorum, he was sweeping his top hat from his head.

'Might we see Lady Fanshawe?' Bowman's moustache twitched. He was sure he could hear the sound of a piano being played.

The footman, an angular young man with a weak chin, nodded in acquiescence and led the two detectives through the hall to a high-ceilinged drawing room. 'You will have to extinguish your pipe,' said the footman to Inspector Hicks. 'Lady Fanshawe cannot abide smoking in the house.'

The most arresting feature of the room was a large picture window that gave out onto Hyde Park itself, and flooded the room with light. Tasteful furniture was placed around an imposing fireplace and mantel and it was here that the two men were directed to sit. The piano sounded much louder now, and Bowman fancied he recognised the rise and fall of one of Chopin's concertos. As the footman left the room, Inspector Hicks immediately threw himself upon a low chaise longue that was placed by the window.

'This would be the life, eh, Bowman?' he beamed, drumming his fingers on his not insubstantial belly.

Looking around, Bowman could see the musical motif was continued in the choice of paintings and effects. Oils and lithographs of famous composers hung from the walls and sheet music lay upon a bureau near the door. Bowman placed himself by the fireplace. Though not lit, it provided a natural focus to the room and it was, he thought, the most appropriate position from which to deliver his sad news. Somewhere beyond the room, the sound of the piano came to an abrupt halt. Bowman could hear a low, hurried conversation. A woman's voice was interrupted feverishly by that of a man, though the inspector could not distinguish any words. As footsteps echoed down the hall, Bowman cautioned Inspector Hicks to stand in readiness. With a heave and a grunt, Hicks swung his legs from the chaise longue and stood at the window, nervously turning his hat in his hands.

To say Lady Fanshawe swept into the room would be to make a terrible understatement. She was at once a formidable woman. Her steel-grey hair was piled high on her head and fastened with a pin. Her clear, blue eyes regarded Bowman through pince-nez. She had a heavily powdered face and was bedecked, the inspector noticed, with pearls. They hung from her neck, her ears and her fingers. Her figure was hidden within the folds of a full-skirted dress with elaborately decorated hems and cuffs.

'How may I help you, inspector?' Her voice had an edge that Bowman recognised. It was a note he had heard many a time before when he had called unexpectedly upon a house. It was a note of fearful anticipation.

'Lady Fanshawe, I think it best that you be seated.'

'Oh, Good Lord.' Her hand flew to the pearls around her neck as she arranged herself on a wing-backed chair by the fireplace. 'What can be the matter? Is it Kingdom?'

Bowman wished he could be anywhere but in that room. He noticed Inspector Hicks was avoiding his gaze. 'Lady Fanshawe,' he began, carefully. 'I am afraid I bring you the most terrible news. Inspector Hicks and I have just come from White's Club where, I am sad to say,' he steeled himself, 'that your husband has died.'

Lady Fanshawe sat stock still in her chair. Her hands were rested in her lap and her eyes stared straight ahead. The room seemed thick with the silence. Bowman looked to Inspector Hicks who shuffled nervously from foot to foot. Then, suddenly, Lady Fanshawe crumpled. Her hands flew to her face as she leant forward in her chair. Taking a gulp of air, she lifted her head and screamed to the door.

'Geoffrey!' she wailed, quite unexpectedly. 'Geoffrey!'

Bowman heard the skidding of heels on the parquet floor in the hall and turned to see a man enter at the door, his eyes wide in alarm. So that was the other voice he had heard from the piano room.

'What the Dickens is going on?' demanded the man as he flew to Lady Fanshawe's side. He was wearing a formal frock coat and black waistcoat. The only bit of colour he had permitted about him was the cravat that flashed canary yellow at his throat.

'Geoffrey,' Lady Fanshawe was wailing. 'They say that Kingdom is dead!'

A look of incomprehension passed over the man's face as he rose. 'Would you please do me the honour of explaining just what has happened?'

'And who might you be?' boomed Hicks from the window. He had clearly, for reasons unknown to Bowman, taken offence at the man's demeanour.

'I am Geoffrey Warburton,' the man replied with a guarded tone. 'Lady Fanshawe's music teacher.' Bowman thought he was being a little over-careful. Hicks raised his eyebrows. 'And friend,' Warburton clarified.

'I am afraid to say that Sir Kingdom Fanshawe collapsed and died in the club's lounge just forty-five minutes ago.' Bowman kept his eye on Lady Fanshawe as he spoke. She was beyond speaking now, her whole body shaking as her grief engulfed her. Warburton knelt again and took her hand. 'Is he still there?'

'The body has been taken to Charing Cross Hospital to be examined.'

'Examined?' keened Lady Fanshawe, a handkerchief at her face.

'Do you suspect foul play?' Warburton's eyes flitted between the two detectives, searching for clues.

'There is a detail in his death,' began Bowman, 'that may be of interest, that is all.'

'What will I do without him?' Lady Fanshawe staggered to her feet, her face a mask of distress. 'Oh, Geoffrey, he is dead!'

Warburton moved swiftly to her side as her legs gave way beneath her. 'Inspector,' he pleaded, 'would you offer some assistance?'

Bowman sprang across the room, helping to lead Lady Fanshawe to the chaise longue by the window. There she collapsed, breathing hard.

'Pocock!' Warburton called. The footman appeared at the door suspiciously quickly, thought Bowman. He had clearly been listening from the hall.

'Fetch Lady Fanshawe's smelling salts from the vanity table in her parlour.' He was fanning the poor lady's face with his handkerchief. 'And be quick about it!'

Bowman shared a look with Inspector Hicks. It was most unusual, they were clearly both thinking, that a music teacher should have intimate knowledge of the contents of a lady's parlour.

'She is much given to fainting fits,' Warburton explained. 'On account of a childhood condition.' Bowman nodded slowly.

As Warburton mopped at the lady's forehead, Hicks loped to the window. Throwing up the sash to admit some air, he turned back into the room and fixed Warburton with an accusing stare.

'Mr Warburton,' he boomed in a voice far too loud for the room. 'Just how long have you been Lady Fanshawe's music teacher?'

'Some five years,' Warburton stammered. 'She is progressing well.'

'And what was your opinion of Sir Kingdom Fanshawe?'

Lady Fanshawe bawled again at Hicks' use of the past tense. Warburton rose to his feet, clearly rattled.

'I have found him to be nothing but civil. Though perhaps a little absent.'

'He was often at the club?' Bowman was attempting a more conciliatory tone.

'Too often, in my opinion.'

'Geoffrey!' snapped Lady Fanshawe, suddenly alert.

'Lady Fanshawe,' began Bowman as he knelt beside the chaise longue. 'Are you quite recovered?'

Wiping her nose on her handkerchief, the lady of the

house nodded slowly. 'I am, inspector,' she sniffed. 'Please forgive my distress.'

'I would expect nothing less, Lady Fanshawe,' Inspector Bowman soothed.

Even though she was calmer now, the unfortunate lady on the chaise longue still took involuntary gulps of air as she spoke. 'You mentioned a detail in my husband's death that provoked suspicion,' she shuddered. 'What detail?'

Bowman swallowed hard as he thought how best to proceed. 'Lady Fanshawe, would you consider your husband a fit man?'

She nodded emphatically. 'He had the strength of a bull, inspector.'

'And he has not recently complained of being in ill health?'

'He has not. For a man of fifty-nine, I should say he was in excellent health.'

'It is unusual,' Hicks offered, none too carefully, 'for such a man to drop down dead.'

Bowman rolled his eyes at his fellow inspector's lack of tact.

'Unusual and most unfortunate,' agreed Warburton, sadly.

'The doorman at White's sent a boy to Scotland Yard on account of his witnessing the events surrounding Sir Kingdom's unfortunate death.'

'What events?' Warburton's eyes narrowed.

'Upon admittance to the club, Sir Kingdom seemed in good health, but the doorman noticed he was rubbing at his neck.'

Warburton shook his head. 'Is that the detail to which you alluded, inspector? It hardly seems relevant at all.'

'It is merely but one link in a chain of events, Mr Warburton,' Bowman asserted, 'that culminated in Sir Kingdom's death.' The inspector turned his full attention on Lady Fanshawe as he related the details of her husband's final moments. 'He staggered to the mantelpiece and there he arched his back as if in spasm.'

'How dreadful,' moaned Lady Fanshawe. 'My poor, poor Kingdom.'

'He was seen to froth at the mouth as he fell, and his death was almost instant.'

There was silence as Bowman concluded, and he could tell that both Lady Fanshawe and her music teacher were each considering the implications.

'Inspector Bowman,' began Warburton, faltering. 'I am not familiar with the passage of a soul into death. Is such a detail unusual?'

'I should say so,' bellowed Hicks from the window. 'Unless the soul in question has been poisoned.'

Bowman sighed and raised a hand to stop Hicks from saying any more.

'Poisoned?' exclaimed Lady Fanshawe, her eyes wide in disbelief.

'It has yet to be confirmed, Lady Fanshawe,' offered Bowman. 'But that is why your husband's body is even now on its way for examination at Charing Cross.' He took a breath. 'Such a death is indeed consistent with one who has been poisoned.'

'And that is why we were called upon,' concluded Hicks, his empty pipe clamped between his teeth as if that were the end of the matter.

'Lady Fanshawe,' Bowman continued, frowning at Hicks' interjection, 'I'm afraid I must ask you this. Is there any reason why anyone might wish your husband dead?'

Lady Fanshawe took a moment to gaze through the window to the park beyond. A pair of young lovers were launching a kite, laughing gaily as it sailed into the air. A costermonger was setting up a barrow to sell his wares. Businessmen were rushing home in their frock coats and top hats. 'There cannot be anyone out of this window,' she mused sadly as she gazed through the glass, 'that has not been touched in some way by the decisions my husband has made in life, either as a soldier or a broker. He has made much of himself, inspector. A man with such influence and such means can scarcely go through life without making enemies.'

Bowman nodded slowly.

'Do you really have no idea who might have done such a thing?' Warburton blinked.

'We must first ascertain the man's movements,' blustered Hicks. 'Then we might discover who had the opportunity, the means and the motive.' He said this last straight at Warburton, as if accusing the man himself.

Bowman took his notebook and pencil from his pocket. 'Lady Fanshawe, could you enlighten us as to Sir Kingdom's movements today?'

'Of course, inspector. He rose and spent the morning

with me, attending to his correspondence.'

'And what time did you arrive, Mr Warburton?'

'On the dot of eleven as I do every day.'

'Every day?' parroted Hicks meaningfully, his arms folding across his chest.

'Yes, inspector. Lady Fanshawe is an excellent pupil, and one does not attain excellence but through regular practice.'

'And I take it Sir Kingdom had left before you arrived?' Hicks leered. His meaning was clear.

'Yes, inspector,' Warburton said bravely, a note of defiance in his voice. 'We have been quite alone all afternoon.'

'The footman at White's said he did not come to the club until a little after half past two. Where did your husband go before this?'

Lady Fanshawe propped herself up on one elbow. 'He was due to dine at the Hackney Union Workhouse.'

From the corner of his eye, Bowman noticed Inspector Hicks flinch where he stood. Turning to his companion, he saw the bluff inspector staring innocently back, a weak smile playing about his lips. He raised his eyebrows.

'He is - ' Lady Fanshawe swallowed as she corrected herself. '*Was* the prime benefactor there, although I believe he was to withdraw his support today.'

'Was that common knowledge?' Bowman asked.

'He had told not another soul, inspector, just me. We had absolute trust in one another,' said Lady Fanshawe looking pointedly at Inspector Hicks. 'And that went for his financial matters, too. What was his business, was my business.'

'Then,' spluttered Hicks, suddenly, 'that is where we must begin our investigations.' Bowman couldn't help but notice that Hicks seemed suddenly perturbed. 'Bowman,' he pronounced as he made for the door, 'I will hail us a hansom.'

'No need, inspector,' said Lady Fanshawe. 'I shall have my driver put at your disposal.'

At that very moment, Pocock the footman entered the room with a small vial in his hands. 'Your smelling salts, my lady,' he said with a reverential dip of his head.

'Oh, don't be silly, Pocock,' Lady Fanshawe snapped. 'It's not smelling salts I want, it's answers.' Pocock let his hand drop. 'And Inspector Bowman here is the only man qualified enough to get them for me.' Pocock threw a look to the inspector. Bowman gave a nervous smile and smoothed his moustache between his forefinger and thumb. 'Be sure that Pedley is put at his disposal. The inspectors wish to be taken to the Hackney Workhouse.'

Pocock bowed low. 'Of course,' he purred. Turning sharply about, he left the room to fetch Pedley from the kitchens where he was teasing the cook.

Lady Fanshawe now felt strong enough to rise to her feet. 'Inspector Bowman,' she began, grabbing at Warburton's arm for support, 'I charge you to find my husband's killer.'

The carriage was a grand affair but, however comfortable the ride, Inspector Bowman felt keenly aware that the last person to sit in his place was now a dead man.

Sir Kingdom Fanshawe clearly enjoyed the finer things in life. The seats were well upholstered, the wood polished to a shine. The carriage was pulled through the streets by two handsome bay mares and driven impeccably by Pedley, a smart and officious-looking coachman. The sun was setting now and the shadows lengthening. Bowman cast a sideways glance at Inspector Hicks as he sat beside him. He had never seen the portly inspector so introspective. He had spoken not a word throughout the whole journey, but rather had sat, solid and still. If felt to Bowman that the man was deliberately trying to avoid his gaze, and any attempts to discuss their progress were met with a moody silence. Throughout the duration of the journey to Hackney, Hicks simply stared out of the window, absently gnawing his lip and stroking his beard.

At last, Hackney Union Workhouse hove into view. It was an imposing sprawl of a building. Tall, rectangular windows stared balefully from its austere walls. There was little by way of embellishment or decoration, noted Bowman as the carriage drew to a stop outside its gates, giving the building a rather austere, forbidding air. As he stepped from the carriage footplate, the inspector fancied he could hear an altercation from within the workhouse walls. Turning to Hicks, he saw the rotund inspector had strode ahead, his head down, his hands jammed into the pockets of his long coat. Even his pipe was absent. He looked, Bowman mused, quite out of sorts.

The gates were opened by a skeletal-looking man with a thin mouth. After sharply enquiring as to the nature of the inspectors' visit, he introduced himself as Courtney

Ambrose, the workhouse caretaker. Bowman had been reticent to divulge the details of their call, saying only that he was pursuing some enquiries concerning Sir Kingdom Fanshawe. Ambrose shot the inspector a look of concern, then bade the two men follow him across the yard to the main building. Throughout all this, Bowman noticed, the usually ebullient Inspector Hicks spoke not a word.

'The master is in the male ward, trying to settle the inmates for the evening,' intoned Ambrose ominously as they walked. Bowman's frown cut deep into his forehead. He had never before set foot inside a workhouse, but there was something about the place that seemed to him dreadfully familiar. It was there in the looming towers and blank windows. Even the signs about the place seemed to mock him; 'To The Wards', 'Matron's Office' and 'Infirmary'. Looking closer as he was led through the yard, Bowman noticed the brickwork was crumbling at the corners. He saw windows that were cracked or missing their glass entirely. Wooden sills had been left to rot and paint peeled from doors. What greenery there was about the place grew in wild, unruly clumps. All in all, thought Bowman, the workhouse and its grounds were subject to a general air of neglect.

Ducking through a low door, Ambrose motioned that the two inspectors should follow him into the ward. Already, Bowman could hear the cacophony within. As they entered the ward, he could see it was little more than a dormitory. Four lines of low, wooden-framed beds stretched away to the furthest wall. Lamps hung at intervals from the rafters, affording the room a sickly glow in the fading light of day. What windows there were, Bowman noticed, only looked out onto other walls of further buildings outside. As the workhouse had grown, he surmised, little thought had been given to the views afforded to the unfortunate inmates. Most arresting of all, however, was the sight of a hundred or more inmates crowded round a bed in the middle of the room. A long-limbed, sinewy-looking man sat on the mattress chewing on a matchstick, his face a mask of defiance. Voices, and several fists, were raised in protest. Amongst the throng stood a small man with a trim moustache, his hands raised in a gesture of exasperation. Improbably, he was wearing the most garish green frock coat the inspector had ever seen, only surpassed by his sickly yellow spats. Bowman supposed this must be the master of the workhouse.

'You must understand,' he was saying, 'that I do not make the rules.'

'Then if you do not make 'em,' a rough-looking man with a full beard responded, 'where's the harm in you breakin' 'em?' There was a roar of approval from the men around him.

'The Board of Guardians would hear of it,' appealed the master, 'And then where should I be?'

'Out on yer ear, wiv a bit of luck!' chimed the man from the bed. The hall erupted in laughter at this, and the man fell back on his mattress with a look of satisfaction on his face.

'I'm sure he won't be a moment,' Ambrose whispered. Bowman nodded in understanding and stole a look to Inspector Hicks. He was looking carefully around the room, as if in expectation of seeing something in particular. Catching Bowman's eye, he fained a sudden interest in proceedings.

'Gibbons must be placed in solitary confinement for the rest of the week,' the master was opining, 'as fit punishment for his behaviour in the breaking yard.' There was jeering from the crowd as he fought to make his point. 'I will not have my staff spoken to in such a manner.'

The man with the beard stood toe to toe with him now, the diminutive master's eyes at chest height. 'Unless you remove that punishment,' he was snarling as he looked down upon the master's head, 'we shall do a lot worse to your staff than speak to them in such a manner.' There were murmurs of agreement from his fellow inmates. 'We shall split their heads with the stones we break in the breaking yard!'

There was much cheering and stamping of feet as the man concluded his threats, and the master was left in no doubt as to the seriousness of the situation. He seemed to visibly shrink. Swallowing hard, he ran his fingers through his hair. His lower lip wobbling, he was plainly considering his position. 'Very well,' he said at last, a quiver in his voice. 'I shall overlook it this once.' There was a deafening roar from the men. The master hurried away towards the door in an effort to effect his escape. Turning as he fled, he attempted a final show of authority. 'But I shall not tolerate further dissent!' The jeers continued and were joined with cries of 'Get out!', 'Leave us!' and, somewhat more ominously, 'Come again and see what you get!'

As he turned to leave, the master ran headlong into Inspector Bowman. Regaining his balance, he looked to Ambrose, blinking in an expression of enquiry.

'Mr Barrett, sir,' Ambrose shouted over the din, 'these gentlemen are from Scotland Yard.'

Ferdinand Barrett was visibly more relaxed in his own quarters. He threw himself into his chair and gestured that Bowman and Hicks might each pull up their own. Bowman noticed that even Inspector Hicks declined. Instead, he paced the room like some wild animal, stopping only to stare out the windows to the yard beneath.

'Mr Barrett, I am afraid I bring news of Sir Kingdom Fanshawe.'

'What news?' enquired the diminutive master from his chair. 'He dined with us only this afternoon.'

Bowman cleared his throat. 'Following his meeting with you today, he collapsed and died in the lounge of his club.' He was watching Ferdinand Barrett carefully.

'But that is awful, inspector.' The master rose to his feet and turned to the picture above the mantel. It was a representation of a forest glade and Barrett would often imagine himself walking in its dappled light when he needed an escape from the world. From behind, it was impossible to see just how Barrett had taken the news. Bowman looked for any sign of a reaction in the master's narrow shoulders. When he turned, at last, back into the room, he had a look of realisation upon his face. 'What will become of the workhouse?' he asked, simply.

Bowman looked at him, sternly. 'You have not enquired as to how he met his death.' His moustache twitched on his upper lip.

Barrett was at once his fawning self. 'Of course, inspector,' he smiled. 'Forgive me. Just how did Sir Kingdom die?'

By now, thought Bowman as he cast his eyes to his companion, Inspector Hicks would surely have interjected with some facile remark, particularly given Barrett's rather selfish behaviour. The inspector, however, spoke not a word. Indeed, he seemed not to be even listening. Bowman took a breath. 'Early indications would point to him being poisoned.'

'Poisoned?' gasped Barrett, falling to his chair again, 'Then he was murdered?'

'Lady Fanshawe says Sir Kingdom was due to dine with you today.'

'Yes, he did,' Barrett confirmed. 'He takes monthly luncheons with the staff. It is our opportunity to keep him apprised of progress here at the workhouse. As our prime benefactor, it is his perfect right.'

'Where do these luncheons occur?' Bowman raised his eyebrows.

'Why, right here, inspector,' blinked Barrett, innocently. 'In these very rooms.'

Bowman looked about him. The master's rooms were wide and spacious with high ceilings. They were, he suspected, the nearest to opulence one was likely to find in the entirety of the workhouse buildings. There was no sign here of cracked windows or rotting sills. Indeed, the rooms seemed very well maintained, with tasteful paper on the walls and new rugs upon the floor. There were three rooms in all, Bowman could see. The parlour stood at one end of the building, with the master's bedroom at the other. In between was the dining room. It was furnished with a decorated Welsh dresser and a long, oval table fashioned from walnut. The master had clearly got very used to the luxuries and comforts his position afforded him.

'Then this must be the very table,' Bowman remarked as he walked into the dining room.

'Indeed so,' confirmed Barrett as he watched Bowman pull a notebook from his pocket.

'And just who, besides yourself and Sir Kingdom, took luncheon here today?'

Barrett licked his lips. 'Well, there was Ambrose the caretaker, whom I know you have met already.' Bowman made a note with the stub of a pencil. 'The ward superintendent, William Mooney, sat next to him.' Barrett was clearly imagining them in their positions as he spoke. 'Then came Robert Coldman, the labour superintendent,' Barrett cast his eyes at the final chair. 'Then finally, next to him and to Sir Kingdom's right hand, sat our matron, Florence Habgood.'

From the corner of his eye, Bowman saw Hicks flinch momentarily. He seemed then to freeze and stand stock still, as if afraid of displaying any emotion at all.

'Are your private kitchens beneath this room?' asked Bowman as he turned his attention back to the matter in hand.

'They are, inspector.'

'And just what time did you sit down to dine?'

'At a little after midday.' A dawning realisation settled on Barrett's features. 'But, inspector,' he spluttered, 'you can't believe - '

'According to the footman at White's Club, Sir Kingdom Fanshawe met his death at half past two.'

Barrett's mouth hung agape. He clutched at a chair for support as the implications became clear in his mind.

'But,' he stammered. 'That's impossible!'

'Oh?' Inspector Bowman raised his eyebrows,

'How so?'

'Well,' Barrett was thinking quickly, 'surely it would take time for any poison to take effect?'

'There is a poison that will take effect within two hours if delivered in a sufficient dose.'

'But that would mean - ' Barnett collapsed into the nearest chair. 'That would mean he was poisoned at this meal.'

Inspector Bowman snapped his notebook shut. 'Indeed it would, Mr Barrett,' he confirmed. 'Might I ask that you call all who ate at this table today back into this room?'

Barrett nodded, slowly, rising from his chair. 'Yes, of course.' The colour had drained from his face.

'Where might we find the matron?' Inspector Bowman was surprised to hear the voice behind him. Turning, he saw Inspector Hicks leaning forward on his feet in anticipation of the answer. Bowman thought it odd that he had chosen just this moment to speak and such a seemingly innocuous question.

'At this hour, she would be in the infirmary about her rounds,' the master offered.

'Then I shall fetch her myself.' With that, the rotund inspector bowled from the room at speed, his coat tails billowing behind him as he bounded down the stairs. From the window, Bowman could see him loping across the yard, stopping only to read a sign that pointed him in the way of the infirmary. He strode off between two larger buildings and out of sight. Bowman then saw the diminutive figure of the master following, his tasteless cravat fluttering at his neck. He seemed even smaller from Bowman's vantage, shaking his head disbelief as he flitted from building to building in search of his staff.

In a matter of minutes he was striding back across the yard to his rooms. The caretaker Bowman had met at the gates followed in his wake, together with two other men whom the inspector took to be Mooney and Coldman. They followed the master almost step for step. At the same time, Inspector Hicks suddenly appeared from the corner in the company of a slight, weak-looking woman in an apron. Strangely, Bowman noticed, they seemed to be in the midst of an animated conversation.

As one by one they were seated around the table, Bowman took the opportunity to look from one to the other. Young Mooney seemed most ill at ease as he fidgeted with his shirt cuffs. Coldman sat bolt upright, his eyebrows raised in expectation. Old Ambrose rested his elbows on the table. The matron's demeanour was most strange of all, Bowman noticed. She would periodically glance to Inspector Hicks, almost involuntarily.

They all took the news of Sir Kingdom's death with the customary surprise, Bowman noted, each expressing their shock at the turn of events. As it became clear, however, just how the knight had met his death and Bowman expressed his suspicions at to the cause, the assembled company fell into an uneasy silence. The implication was quite clear. One of them was responsible for Sir Kingdom's murder. Almost at once, Bowman could see them eyeing each other with suspicion.

'But which of us would have the motive for such a thing?' asked Robert Coldman boldly.

'Lady Fanshawe has told us,' said Bowman thoughtfully, with reference to his notebook, 'That Sir Kingdom intended to give you notice today, that he was to withdraw his financial support form the workhouse.'

'And so he did,' mumbled Mooney as he fidgeted. 'As we ate.'

Barrett leaned in from where he sat, holding the inspector in his gaze. 'But surely you don't think his murder is connected to the fact?'

'Who would lose the most if Sir Kingdom's money was withdrawn?' Inspector Bowman leant against the Welsh dresser.

'We would all lose, inspector,' chimed Florence Habgood from her chair. 'Sir Kingdom's money has kept the workhouse open these last two years.'

'But, inspector,' Barrett was thinking hard, 'what would Sir Kingdom's murder achieve? Unless there was provision made in his will, I assume his money would cease with his death.'

Bowman attempted to wrestle back control of proceedings. 'Just who cooked the meal, Mr Barrett?' Again, there was an uneasy silence in the room.

'I did.' Florence Habgood's eyes looked more tired than ever as she spoke. 'I cooked the food as I always do.'

From the corner of his eye, Bowman saw Hicks lift his hands to his face in a curious gesture.

'I do not trust the cook to provide adequately for so distinguished a guest,' Mrs Habgood continued, 'and so I take it upon myself once a month.'

'Did you have assistance?'

'Only in the serving of it. Young William here helped carry the dishes to the table.' Mooney gulped at her side.

'Then he could have poisoned the food on its way to the table,' boomed Hicks, suddenly.

'Inspector Hicks,' rounded Bowman, holding the bluff inspector in his gaze, 'if the food had been poisoned, surely all round this table would have suffered. They all ate the same food.' Hicks blinked.

'And then there is the most pertinent question of all.'

'And just what is that?' Hicks asked defensively, planting his hands on his hips.

Bowman turned to Robert Coldman. He had been watching proceedings intently from his chair. 'Mr Coldman,' began the inspector, 'at what point in the meeting did Sir Kingdom mention he was withdrawing his funds?'

Coldman's eyes took on a faraway look as he thought

back to the events surrounding the meal. 'At pudding,' he said finally. 'Or over his cigar. At the end of the meal, at any rate.'

'So?' blustered Hicks, his eyes wide.

'Inspector Hicks,' explained Bowman with a sigh, 'it is perfectly plain. If Sir Kingdom was poisoned during the meal, then his poisoning must have been for another reason entirely, quite coincidental to the fact of his withdrawing funds. How was anyone around this table to know of his intentions? Lady Fanshawe herself said that he had told no one but her.' Hicks was blinking furiously in confusion. 'I believe Sir Kingdom's statement came as a surprise to all around this table, and yet his fate was already sealed.'

There was another silence in the room.

'Mrs Habgood,' Bowman continued. 'Describe to me your duties as matron here at the workhouse.'

'They are many and varied,' she began, simply. 'From general housekeeping to the supervision of the female inmates and children. Since we lost our doctor, I have also gained responsibility for the health of our inmates.'

'That is purely a temporary measure,' interjected Barrett, defensively.

Bowman took note of the remarks. 'And in the course of those duties, Mrs Habgood,' he continued, 'would you have recourse to certain medicines?'

She nodded slowly, clearly aware of the implication. 'Yes, inspector I would. But none of them are poisons.'

'Ah! Then you would have no objection to me examining your medicine cabinet for an inventory of its contents?' bellowed Hicks, suddenly.

'Certainly not,' Mrs Habgood maintained.

With a look and a nod of the head, Bowman dismissed his fellow inspector. Hicks lifted his coat about him in readiness for the stairs and turned from the room, but not before, Bowman noticed, giving Mrs Habgood a look he found difficult to read.

The Silver Cross Inn was busy as usual. The cold, March air was bringing people off the streets in search of warmth and Harris, the landlord, was deftly passing drinks across the bar to waiting customers.

Bowman had settled himself in his favourite chair by the fire, his coat hanging from a hook on the chimney breast. Gazing through the window to Whitehall beyond, he let his mind wander over the events of the day. Inspector Hicks' behaviour was still troubling him and, try as he might, he could see no reason for it. He had sent the flustering inspector to Doctor Crane at Charing Cross Hospital with his inventory from the infirmary's drug store. It was to be hoped that some match could be made with the poison that saw an end to Sir Kingdom Fanshawe in White's that afternoon. As he pondered over his glass of porter, the door before him swung open and Hicks himself entered.

'First things first, Bowman,' he blustered as he bounded towards the bar, leaving chaos in his wake. The wind from the streets whipped in through the open door, blowing Bowman's hat from his table. Bending to retrieve it, Bowman tapped his fingers impatiently on the brim as

Hicks made his order at the bar. Some minutes later, the portly inspector was squeezing himself into the chair opposite Bowman. A pie steamed from a plate before him and a jar of ale foamed in his hand.

'I have come hot-foot from Charing Cross,' he began as he took a mouthful of his pie. 'I furnished Doctor Crane with the contents of the workhouse infirmary.' He pulled his notebook from his pocket. 'And there was nothing on this list to explain Sir Kingdom's death.'

'Are you sure?' Bowman asked, his frown creasing deep on his forehead.

'I am certain,' boomed Hicks as he wiped some gravy from his beard with a sleeve. 'The doctor has discovered proof of poisoning by strychnine, a toxin that does not appear on this list, and so was not present in the drug store at Hackney Workhouse.' He snapped his notebook shut as if to indicate the end of the conversation and lifted his jar to take a deep draft of his ale.

Bowman was bemused. 'The purchase of strychnine is very heavily regulated. I doubt anyone about that table would have the means to procure it privately.'

'Then perhaps Sir Kingdom was not poisoned at the workhouse,' Hicks twinkled.

'That would certainly seem to be the case,' said Bowman, his moustache twitching. He had noticed a sudden change in his fellow inspector's disposition. Now suspicion had been lifted from anyone at the workhouse, Hicks appeared more carefree in his demeanour. Bowman sighed. 'We must go back to Lady Fanshawe and ascertain her husband's whereabouts for the last few days.' Just as he stood to collect his coat from the hook, the door flew open again to admit a tall young man with an open face and a mop of curly blonde hair.

'Inspector Bowman,' panted Sergeant Graves as he fought to close the door against the wind. 'I have been sent to find you.'

'What is it, Graves?' Bowman was alarmed at Graves' serious expression. To see him in any other but his usual jovial manner gave the inspector cause for concern.

'A murder, sir,' the young sergeant breathed. 'I understand it may be pertinent to your investigations.'

'Spit it out, man,' barked Bowman from the fireplace. 'What is it?'

'It's Lady Fanshawe, sir. She's been found dead.'

Lady Fanshawe was slumped at her piano in the music room, a slick of blood dripping from her neck onto the piano keys and from there to the floor. Geoffrey Warburton was standing in the corner, as far away from her body as he could possibly get without actually leaving the room.

'And this is exactly where she was found?'

'Exactly, inspector,' he whimpered. 'I had left the house without my sheet music following Lady Fanshawe's lesson, and so returned this evening to retrieve it.' He was gulping air as he spoke. 'The footman showed me into the drawing room where I was to wait, and then I heard his cry.'

'I found her just as you see her,' said Pocock, the

footman, from the door.

'So she had been practising her piano?' Bowman was trying to establish a sequence of events.

'That's right, sir,' nodded the footman. 'For quite some time after Mr Warburton had left.'

'She was always so conscientious,' offered Warburton, sadly. 'A model pupil.'

'When the music stopped, I assumed she had taken to her daybed.' Pocock pointed to a low couch by the side window. It was richly decorated in lacy chintz and laden with plush, plumped cushions. 'She would often take a sleep before dinner.'

'So, of course, you thought nothing of the silence,' nodded Bowman in understanding.

'It was only when Mr Warburton returned that I had cause to call upon her.'

'Just how did her killer enter the house, Pocock?' Bowman narrowed his eyes as Pocock shuffled uncomfortably where he stood.

'Truth be told, sir, I left the back door open, just for a moment. But it was clearly long enough for the killer to let himself in.' Bowman shook his head in exasperation. 'She could never abide smoking in the house, sir,' continued Pocock by way of an explanation. 'Even Sir Kingdom himself would be sent to the summer house for a cigar.'

'She fancied herself a singer, too,' nodded Warburton in confirmation, 'And had long believed the smoke would affect her voice.'

Bowman turned to face Pocock where he stood. 'And

you cannot see the back door from the summer house?'

Pocock nodded. 'That's right, sir. It is angled away from the house so as to afford a view of the fountain.'

'It is a magnificent fountain,' added Warburton.

Bowman approached the body at the piano. Lady Fanshawe had fallen victim to a garrotting. The sound of the piano had covered her assailant's approach so that, Bowman imagined, the first she knew of her fate was the feel of the wire at her neck. Surely, he reasoned, the two deaths must be connected. How else to explain why a man and his wife should both be murdered within hours of each other? Bowman stroked his moustache between his thumb and forefinger as he spoke. 'Who on Earth should want Lady Fanshawe dead, as well as her husband? And why?'

The answer to his second question, at least, came in the form of a cry from Detective Sergeant Graves upstairs. He had been searching the house for further clues and now stood at the top of the wide staircase that led from the hall to the first floor. 'Inspector Bowman, sir,' he called. 'There's something here I think you should see.'

Sir Kingdom's study was a room to behold. Pictorial representations of various military campaigns adorned the wood-panelled walls, and trophy cabinets held collections of medals and weaponry through the ages.

Sergeant Anthony Graves was standing by a picture of the Charge of the Light Brigade at Balaclava as Inspector Bowman entered the room, Warburton and Pocock trailing behind him. The inspector glanced briefly around the room to get his bearings before joining his sergeant by the far wall.

'What is it, Graves?'

'This, sir.' Raising a hand, Graves swung the picture aside on a hinge to reveal a small safe hidden in the wall behind.

'It's been broken into,' said Bowman quietly, as he moved closer to inspect its contents. The door had indeed been prised open, and hung loose on its hinges at an awkward angle.

'Easy enough to do with these old models,' Graves confirmed, his eyes bright. 'All you'd need is a good jemmy.'

Bowman nodded. Safe technology had improved over the past few years, but safe owners had been slow to keep up. The inspector often mused that, for every ten safes kept in London, perhaps as many as six of them would struggle to keep anything safe at all.

'I don't understand,' commented Warburton from the door. 'If the murderer was an opportunist, as we might believe from the fact he entered by a conveniently open door, why would he not simply take his share of the spoils?' Warburton walked to a display cabinet by the window. It contained a collection of medals and memorabilia from the Crimean campaigns. 'These alone would collect a pretty penny,' he cooed.

'I do not believe the killer was an opportunist, Mr Warburton. The fact that he knew where this safe was would speak to him having intimate knowledge of Sir Kingdom's study.' Bowman looked around the walls.

'None of the other paintings have been displaced which

would suggest he headed straight for this picture, knowing the safe was behind it.'

The inspector reached carefully into the safe. Feeling around with his fingers, he pulled out various papers and a box file, placing them all carefully on the large desk by the window.

'He left much behind,' Bowman muttered, almost to himself. 'Which means he had come for something very specific.'

Graves was leafing through the loose pages on the desk. 'These are financial contracts,' he was saying. 'Beyond me, but they seem to be for loans and investments.'

Bowman was flipping through the box file. 'There are smudges of blood on the paper,' he said aloud. 'From the killer's hands no doubt.'

'Then he killed Lady Fanshawe first,' nodded Graves.

Inspector Bowman's attention was fixed on the object at his fingers. It was a sturdy box with compartments divided into the letters of the alphabet. The word 'Loans' had been stamped on its cover. Papers and documents bulged from all the compartments but one. Warburton and Pocock drew nearer the desk as Bowman turned it for all to see. Even Queen Victoria herself seemed to lower her eyes from the wall.

Sergeant Graves was the first to speak aloud what they all saw.

'There's a whole letter missing!'

Bowman prised the section apart with his fingers to reveal that the section marked with a 'B' in the file was completely empty. There was a silence in the room as each of the men entertained their own separate thoughts.

'It's unlikely that Sir Kingdom would have no entries in the 'B' section, when every other letter of the alphabet is well represented.'

'Saving 'X' and 'Z', as you might expect,' added Bowman, peering into the box file as he spoke.

'Not quite, sir,' Graves was reaching deep into the file to retrieve a small slip of paper. 'A receipt for a loan to Thomas Xavier,' he read triumphantly.

Pocock was scratching his head, his weak features creased in thought. 'Why would he take all the 'B's?'

'The documents in that section, or some of them at least, must have incriminated him in some matter.'

'Then why not just take the papers that implicated him? Why take them all?' Pocock leaned awkwardly on the desk as he spoke. 'If he had just taken his own, we might never have noticed.' The men in the room turned to Bowman.

'Imagine you were the intruder,' the inspector began, his eyes narrowing as he thought his way through the conundrum. 'You could have been discovered at any moment.' He looked at the footman. 'You might only have a matter of minutes while Pocock smoked his cigarette in the summer house.'

'I wish to God I'd never had that blasted cigarette,' muttered Pocock, guiltily.

'Far quicker,' continued Bowman, 'to simply grab a whole section of the file, than to leaf through individual pages to find the relevant documents.'

'Then why not take the whole file?' Graves was blinking

as he thought.

In response, Bowman lifted the file and dropped it in Graves' arms. 'Because it's heavy, Graves, and cumbersome.' The sergeant nodded in confirmation to the other men. 'Far easier to take and dispose of a few pages rather than a whole box file.'

Geoffrey Warburton walked to the window to look out over Hyde Park. The open vista and airy spaces beyond gave him a sense of order and calm amidst the chaos and disorder of his day. 'If Lady Fanshawe was at her piano,' he said at last, 'And the assailant had made his entry unheard, why did he go to the trouble of murdering her?' Warburton baulked at the memory of her body in the music room, slumped ignominiously over her piano.

'Because he feared discovery?' offered Graves, 'She might have stopped at any moment.'

'There is a great jump, Sergeant Graves,' Bowman opined, 'between being an opportunist thief and a murderer. In my experience the one hardly ever leads to the latter.' He drummed his fingers on the desk as he spoke. 'No,' he said eventually. 'He gained entry with the express intent of both killing Lady Fanshawe and taking the papers.'

'Why?' gasped Warburton, his eyes wide with the horror of it all.

'When I broke the news of her husband's death to Lady Fanshawe this afternoon, she intimated that they kept no secrets from each other. What was his business, was my business, I believe were her exact words.' Bowman smoothed his moustache between his fingers. 'I think the killer knew that, too. If he was to escape detection, he needed both to dispose of those papers and to dispose of Lady Fanshawe.'

'But, Inspector Bowman,' Warburton breathed, his jaw gripped tight to contain a well of emotion. 'Who could do such things?'

Bowman turned to face him, the light from the window lending a defiant gleam to his eyes. 'A man with much to lose,' he said simply.

The staff had been summoned to the table again, clearly all annoyed at having been called from their rooms so late. Florence Habgood sat in the master's dining room looking smaller than before. She kept her eyes cast down, Inspector Bowman noticed as he surveyed the scene before him. To her right sat William Mooney, as fidgety as ever. Ambrose the caretaker sat in his usual place, leaning his chin upon a skeletal hand, whilst next to him, Robert Coldman tapped his foot as if he had better places to be. Finally, Ferdinand Barrett sat at the head of the table, staring straight ahead. His demeanour was in marked contrast to when they had last met, observed Bowman. Gone was the sycophantic smile and ingratiating manner, replaced with a worried brow and empty gaze. Inspector Hicks stood ominously close to Mrs Habgood, his eyes flicking occasionally to the back of her head. Finally, Sergeant Graves was stood next to Bowman, his notebook at the ready. The assembled company had reacted to the news of Lady Fanshawe's death with much alarm.

'Talk me through the details of the meal again, if you

would, Mr Coldman.'

'It is late, inspector,' Coldman harrumphed. 'Surely, your time would be better spent in pursuit of the murderer than in requesting the details of the menu.'

'Just the timings would do,' snapped Bowman.

Letting go a sigh, Coldman recounted the afternoon's events as best as he remembered them. 'Sir Kingdom arrived for dinner at midday. We were summoned to this room a little earlier, but Mr Barrett was delayed due to an altercation in the breaking yard.' Barrett listened dispassionately. 'Mrs Habgood provided us with the usual fare,' Coldman continued, choosing his words with care. 'And we proceeded through the meal in virtual silence.'

Bowman looked around the table as Coldman spoke. All were listening intently. As Coldman mentioned Mrs Habgood preparing the meal, the inspector thought he saw Hicks flinch, as if he were about to place a hand on the woman's shoulder. Catching Bowman's eye, he quickly placed his hand in his pocket in a studied display of nonchalance.

'It was only at the end of the meal that we engaged in conversation, with reference made to the new wall in the inmates' privy. Sir Kingdom was not impressed and so chose the moment to inform us of his intent to withdraw his financial support.'

'Thank you, Mr Coldman,' Bowman nodded. He looked to Graves to see that he was busy capturing the salient details with a scratch of his pencil.

'We have established, have we not,' Bowman began, 'that the poisoning was not as a response to Sir Kingdom's news. How could it be when he only revealed his intentions after the meal? But there is something you have neglected to mention, Mr Coldman.' Coldman stared, blankly. 'Everyone around the table partook of the same food.'

'We have established that already, Bowman,' thundered Hicks, his great beard bristling before him. 'This exonerates Mrs Habgood of any hand in the affair.'

'Possibly,' agreed Bowman, again concerned at his fellow inspector's strange behaviour. 'But there is a small detail that Mr Coldman has omitted.' He turned again to the labour superintendent. 'What exactly happened at the end of the meal?'

Coldman repeated his earlier assertion with a weary look. 'It's really very simple, inspector,' he sighed. 'Sir Kingdom sat in that very chair with his cigar and told us of his decision.'

'Precisely,' said Bowman, a look of triumph on his face. 'And did anyone else partake of a cigar?'

Ambrose the caretaker was folding his arms, pointedly. 'None of us was offered one,' he said.

'You mentioned the cigar in our earlier conversation, Mr Coldman,' continued Bowman. 'But you neglected to mention just whose cigar it was.'

Slowly, everyone turned to the occupant in the chair at the head of the table. Ferdinand Barrett's eyes widened in protestation.

'You are suggesting I poisoned Sir Kingdom with a cigar?' he laughed. 'The very idea is preposterous!'

'Not so preposterous when one examines the details,'

Bowman asserted, rounding on the small man in the chair. 'The poison could not have been in the food as everyone partook of every dish. Even the wine would be shared.' He looked around the table at the nodding heads.

'The wine was from a carafe,' chimed Mooney, his face alive with the realisation. 'We shared everything but the cigars.'

'Mr Barrett, I would suggest you poisoned the cigars you passed to Sir Kingdom Fanshawe at the end of the meal.'

There were gasps from the assembled staff at the boldness of Bowman's accusation.

'This is ridiculous,' Barrett complained. 'How could I be certain which cigar he would choose?'

Bowman's audience turned towards him in expectation of his response. 'You could not,' he said, calmly. 'And therefore, I expect you poisoned them all. It would be a simple matter. And it would explain why you did not offer the cigars to anyone else.'

'How could you?' Florence Habgood cried, her hands at her face. 'What would you hope to gain?'

'Ferdinand Barrett hoped to escape financial ruin, Mrs Habgood,' the inspector continued, his eyes fixed firmly on the master of the workhouse. Barrett sat in stony stillness. 'And that silence, Mr Barrett,' Bowman concluded, 'speaks volumes.'

'And Lady Fanshawe's death?' blinked the labour superintendent.

'The two events were intimately linked, Mr Coldman.' Bowman was standing at the window now, looking out over the workhouse yard. At this late hour, the inmates should have been confined to their wards, but still the inspector saw one or two gathered to enjoy a smoke in the evening light, a sign of the lack of discipline that reigned within the workhouse walls. 'Sergeant Graves,' began Bowman, 'just what did we find in Sir Kingdom's study?'

Graves cleared his throat. 'A safe had been opened and its contents examined. Certain documents had been stolen, pertaining to loans that Sir Kingdom had made to certain individuals.'

'All the papers from a section marked 'B' had been taken. Mr Barrett,' said Bowman, turning back into the room. 'I believe those documents incriminated you, and that is why you took them.'

The assembled company were shocked again. 'Is this true?' gasped Florence Habgood.

Bowman bent low to meet Barrett's gaze. 'I believe you were the recipient of a loan or loans from Sir Kingdom Fanshawe, am I correct?'

There was a pause as Barrett studied his hands.

'Yes,' he said at last.

'A loan that you were having trouble repaying?'

'Yes,' repeated Barrett, his voice almost a whisper.

'How much, Ferdinand?' Mrs Habgood was leaning forward on her chair.

Barrett swallowed hard. 'Two hundred pounds,' he said, at last.

'But why kill Lady Fanshawe?' asked Mooney, his mouth agape.

'She would know,' hissed Barrett. 'I had no doubt Sir Kingdom shared with her the news of my defaulting on payments.'

'Indeed,' muttered Coldman. 'Sir Kingdom said only this afternoon that he shared details of his financial affairs only with her.'

'She would betray me during any investigation.'

'You were intending on breaking in but, as luck would have it, you found a door wide open.' Bowman looked stern.

Barrett turned to appeal hopelessly to the inspector, 'A master's wage is next to nothing. Sir Kingdom Fanshawe was my only hope.'

'His loan helped you finance your taste for finer things.' Bowman looked about him. 'The furnishings, the food, the clothes.' Barrett put a hand instinctively to his brocade waistcoat. 'And yet, on a master's wage, you could not repay the loan.'

'He insisted I pay it all with interest or face the consequences. I simply do not have the means.'

Coldman nodded from his chair. 'Sir Kingdom was clearing his books of bad loans and investments, including this workhouse, and you.'

'And so you poisoned him,' Bowman nodded. 'It was pure coincidence that he chose the same day to issue his ultimatum with regard to the workhouse.'

'Inspector,' said Ambrose, suddenly, 'just where is the evidence for any this? Where are the papers he stole, the poison he used?'

'There is no evidence,' insisted Bowman to looks of exasperation. 'Because it was disposed of. Firstly, in the case of the papers, by Mr Barrett himself. And secondly, in the case of the poison, by Inspector Hicks.'

There was another gasp. Jaws hung slack and all heads turned to the rotund inspector. All heads, except that of Florence Habgood. Hicks blinked at the accusation, as if he stood in the full glare of the summer sun.

'Inspector Hicks,' Bowman said slowly. 'Just what is your relationship with Mrs Habgood?'

'I have no idea what you mean,' the portly inspector complained.

'You have been protecting her at every turn.' Inspector Bowman advanced upon his colleague. 'Just what hold does she have over you?'

Unusually, Hicks was lost for words. His mouth opened and shut again as he thought how best to proceed.

'I am his sister,' interjected the matron, quite unexpectedly. 'Ignatius is my older brother.'

Bowman looked to the frail woman at the table. As he peered closer, the likeness became apparent. Though much smaller in stature than her bloated older brother, there were similarities in the eyes and about the nose.

'He was only protecting me from suspicion.'

Bowman stood toe to toe with Inspector Hicks. 'You were obstructing my enquiries,' he seethed.

Hicks took a breath. 'I could not see my sister found guilty of a murder she did not commit,' he spat.

'If she was an innocent party in Sir Kingdom's murder, she would have been found so by a court of law.'

'I have no confidence in the law!' Hicks' voice echoed around the room.

Something in Bowman seemed to snap. He grabbed

Hicks by the lapels of his coat and shoved him back to the wall. 'You serve the law!' he shouted in Hick's face.

'Then perhaps I mean I have no confidence in you.' Hicks pushed back at the inspector and sent him staggering to the table. Bowman gathered himself for a fight, pulling his arm back in anticipation of a swing. His eyes blazed.

'Sir!' The sound of Graves' voice brought him up sharp. Swallowing hard, the inspector lowered his arm and looked around the room. All eyes were upon him. 'Was there strychnine in the infirmary stores?' he panted. The matron nodded. 'Who would have access to it?'

Florence Habgood looked slowly up to the master of the workhouse. 'Only myself and Mr Barrett,' she said, quietly.

'All this would explain your strange behaviour, Hicks,' Bowman mopped at his forehead with a sleeve. 'From the moment you heard of Sir Kingdom's connection to the workhouse in our interview with his wife.'

'I would not see my sister implicated,' Hicks replied, simply.

'And so you volunteered to search the infirmary drug store,' Bowman was nodding. 'Where, no doubt, you found the poison.'

Hicks reached slowly into one of the deeper pockets of his coat. Slowly, dramatically, he produced a small bottle from its folds. It was of brown glass and bore a label; STRYCHNINE.

'Just a grain is enough to kill a man,' Bowman hissed. 'A grain implanted in the tobacco of a cigar would do for a man in a matter of a few hours.' He glared at Hicks. 'You were prepared to see a man get away with murder than see your sister implicated.'

Hicks shrugged. "Sometimes, Bowman, blood is thicker than water.'

'Inspector Hicks,' Bowman snarled. 'I wish you to search that grate for burnt fragments of Barrett's contracts.' He pointed a shaking finger at the fireplace, then turned his furious eyes upon the master of the workhouse. 'Sergeant Graves,' he hissed. 'Take that man away and charge him.'

~

RICHARD JAMES

The next two short stories take place following the events of the second novel in the Bowman Of The Yard series, THE DEVIL IN THE DOCK.

THE HAMPSTEAD GARROTTING

MAY, 1892

From its elevated position, and on a clear day, the London suburb of Hampstead afforded views of Windsor Castle to the west and Leith Hill in Surrey to the south. The dirty sprawl of the city just four miles away could be studiously ignored, its very existence denied, if one wished. The day-tripper could simply turn their attention to the leafy green boulevards and open parks, and their noses to the sweet, clean air that they produced. Small wonder then, that no less a man than Charles Dickens himself proclaimed the area 'one of the best and healthiest of London's lungs'.

Ancient oaks grew on Hampstead Heath, solid and immutable, alongside younger beech and wild service trees, throwing shade on the holly and rowan that crowded at their bases as if for comfort. A walk beneath their canopy could reward the keen observer with glimpses of many an industrious creature, from the humble beetle to the snuffling badger. The hammer of the woodpecker competed with the hoot of the owl, and red kites reared their young in messy nests of sticks and twigs. Poppies grew tall amongst beds of daisies, their fragile, papery petals opening out to the spring sun.

None of this, however, was noticed by the young lad who ran the length of Belsize Crescent. Stopping to retrieve his cap as it slipped from his head, he turned again towards his destination, a look of determination on his face. He slowed his pace to avoid a flower seller as she rounded the corner to the crescent, then turned his heels to the basement rooms of Number Thirty-Two. He leapt over the balustrade to the tiny front garden and almost tripped down the stairs to the door in his haste. The houses in Belsize Crescent boasted five floors of rooms, each storey rented out to those of the professional classes who could afford such surroundings. Hampstead was growing apace but still it was considered a fine place to live.

The young boy stopped at the bottom of the stairs and took a breath. Pulling his trouser legs down to his ankles and straightening his cap, he rapped at the door beneath the steps. He peered in at the window to his right but could see no movement. The room within presented itself in a state of chaos. He could see clothes strewn upon the furniture and shoes scattered by the fire. On a table by the chaise longue, he noticed, a half-empty decanter stood with several glasses, one lying drunkenly on its side. He knocked at the door again, stamping his feet with impatience. Just as he was about to turn back to the road he heard a movement from inside; a shuffling, shambling sound. A key turned in the lock and the door swung open on its hinges. The boy stared at the occupant of the house in disbelief. This wasn't what he had been expecting at all. Before him stood a man in a state of disarray. His shirt was half unbuttoned and his braces hung down around his knees. His hair lay flat on his head. As he stood blinking into the morning sun, it was clear to the lad that the man had only just got up.

'Father Tilcott said you was a Scotland Yarder,' the boy explained. He could scarcely believe it himself. The man in front of him seemed substantial as a shadow.

Bowman rubbed at the beard on his chin as he looked the boy up and down, grunting by way of confirmation. He leaned out of the door to look into the road, keen to be sure there were no other witnesses. He felt embarrassed to be discovered in such a condition.

'What is it?' he rasped, his throat dry.

'You're to come to St. Mary's Chapel,' the boy panted, clearly ill at ease with the situation and the strange man in the doorway.

'Why?' Bowman shook his head to clear the fog on his brain.

'You're to come,' the boy repeated as he began backing away to the steps. 'That's all.' With that, he turned on his heels, clearly believing he had said enough to fulfil whatever demands had been placed upon him.

Bowman stood in the doorway for a moment as if stunned. The conversation had been so brief that, in his addled state, he wondered if it had happened at all. Screwing up his face to restore some feeling, he rubbed his eyes with the back of his hand and yawned. He had barely slept at all. In point of fact, sleep had eluded him for weeks. With a heavy sigh, he stepped back into his room in search of cleaner clothes and closed the door behind him.

Such was the urgency of the summons, he had foregone

a shave. A shirt that he found on the back of a chair had seemed fresh enough and his trousers were serviceable to last another day. Besides, time was clearly of the essence. Jamming his hat on his head as he locked the door behind him, Inspector George Bowman sprang up the steps onto Belsize Crescent, wincing at the throbbing in his head. Around him, smart townhouses stood in rows as if to attention. Painted railings glimmered in the morning sun and ornate brass handles and letterboxes shone from the doors. Swifts wheeled in the sky above him as he strode towards St. Mary's Chapel on Holly Place. Several churchgoers raised their hats to him in greeting. The women, he noticed, averted their eyes. As he rounded the corner, St. Mary's stood before him. It was a plain building, unimposing in its Italianate simplicity. A single bell was peeling from a belcote on the roof. A statue of the Virgin Mary stared balefully out over the empty parkland opposite, the holy infant in her arms. The doors stood open to admit the congregation but Bowman could see that no one was in the mood to enter. Instead, a crowd had gathered at the porch to the chapel, their eyes cast down to the ground at their feet.

'Inspector!' came a voice. 'At last!'

A man in a canon's garb stepped forward from the crowd, his arms spread wide in a curiously pleading gesture. He had a balding head, but had chosen to comb what hair he had over the bare patches. He was tall and thin, his ankles showing beneath his too-short cassock. A long, white sash hung from his neck, trimmed in gold that flashed in the sun as he walked.

'Forgive the rude awakening,' he began, clearly alarmed at Bowman's dishevelled state. 'But I thought it quicker to send the lad to your door than to the police station.'

'Of course,' Bowman nodded. The police station at Rosslyn Hill was a good ten minutes further from his rooms. All the same, he couldn't help but wish the boy had run on and left him to his bed.

'I'm canon here at St. Mary's,' the man was saying, somewhat redundantly. 'My name is Tilcott, Giles Tilcott.' He narrowed his eyes. 'I haven't seen you at chapel, Inspector Bowman, though you are known by some in the congregation.'

'I attend St. John's,' Bowman lied. 'What is the matter?'

'Murder, inspector,' Tilcott replied, plainly. 'That is the matter.'

Bowman's eyebrows rose at the news. 'Where?'

'Right here, at the porch to my chapel.' Turning on his heels, the canon led Bowman through the crowd to the chapel door. The inspector noticed some of the women were sobbing, their handkerchiefs clutched to their noses. Several children, dressed in their Sunday best, were being ushered from the chapel entrance to the road. Bowman caught sight of the lad who had woken him. He regarded the inspector warily as he loitered by the door.

Tilcott came to a halt at the chapel porch, gesturing with his hands that the crowd of onlookers should move back. 'Please,' he implored, 'let us give the inspector room.'

As Bowman looked around at the faces about him, he saw several regard him with suspicion. A lady dressed in a lime green crinoline bent to her husband's ear and whispered the word '*inspector?*' as if in disbelief.

'Detective Inspector George Bowman,' he said pointedly. 'Scotland Yard.' The assertion did nothing to quell the doubtful looks. As the crowd stepped aside, Bowman saw the object of their fascination. There, spread-eagled on the ground, lay the body of a man, a pool of thick, dark blood emanating from a wound at his throat. His legs were spread in a seemingly impossible angle on the flagstones, his hands at his neck. A bunch of keys lay discarded on the path before him. Crouching low to investigate the body, Bowman saw there was a gash on the man's forehead where he had struck the path as he fell. His eyes bulged sightlessly from his skull and his swollen tongue protruded from his mouth. Bowman raised his eyes to the canon who stood with his hands clasped before him, a look of profound sadness on his face.

'His name was Milne,' Tilcott said softly. 'Sartorius Milne. He's the sexton here.'

Bowman nodded. That would explain the formal dress. Milne's frock coat, now stained with blood, was lined with silk, his shoes buffed to a shine.

'Who found the body?' Bowman asked looking around at the assembled crowd.

'I did.' A middle-aged woman stepped from the throng, twisting a handkerchief in her fingers. 'I had come early to practise the Psalms.'

'Miss Bentley is our organist,' Father Tilcott clarified.

'I had expected Mr Milne to have opened the chapel,' the woman continued. 'But found him here just as you see him.'

'Then he has not been moved?'

Miss Bentley shook her head. 'He has not.'

Bowman leaned forward to roll the body onto its back. As he was turned, the wound at Milne's neck opened the wider to expose a tangle of sinew and muscle. There were gasps from the crowd. Irritably, Bowman turned to the gentlemen in the group. 'Might I suggest the ladies be escorted from the chapel grounds?' There was a silence. Alarmingly, Bowman noticed it was the ladies who seemed the most interested of all. They bent in closer to study the body in grisly detail. Even through their tears, the more sensitive of them peered through their fingers at the scene that presented itself.

'Who among you knew this man?' Bowman asked.

'Barely,' coughed a gruff, older man. He had a wide face and a bulbous, purple-veined nose. Bowman noticed his hat was just a little too big for his head. It fell down over the man's bushy eyebrows and flattened the tops of his ears almost comically. 'Mr Milne has not been with us long.'

'Well,' continued Bowman as he reached for the dead man's throat, 'he was clearly garrotted.' To yet more gasps from the crowd, he held up a length of thin wire. It was caked with clots of blood, flesh and sinew. 'And,' he continued as he examined it closely, 'within the hour.' He held the wire up for the canon to see. Tilcott recoiled in horror at the sight. 'See how the blood is yet to set?'

'I've seen enough, Marmaduke,' keened a woman to her

husband. 'Let's go home.'

'Should they not stay, inspector?' asked the canon.

Bowman shook his head, indicating to the lady organist. 'If Miss Bentley found the body and was first at the church, they are no more suspects than anyone else in Hampstead. They may leave if they wish.'

The man led his wife away, comforting her with a kindly arm about her shoulder. The inspector rose slowly to his feet. 'Whoever killed the sexton,' he asserted, 'used an uncommon force.' His eyes met the canon's sad gaze. 'He clearly meant business.'

'What can we do with the poor man?' cried a woman from the crowd. 'It's most unseemly to leave him on the path in the sight of the Virgin.'

Bowman looked up at the alabaster statue of Mary above. She gazed down with sightless eyes, her expression divinely implacable.

'Father Tilcott,' Bowman's moustache twitched at his mouth as he spoke. 'Do you have anywhere we might keep the man?'

Tilcott dipped his head. 'He may be taken through the chapel to the school,' he began, 'if volunteers may be found to carry the man. We have some linen altar cloths that he might be wrapped in.'

Three of the men stepped forward to perform the grisly duty as the canon ducked through the door to the chapel. Bowman noticed all but one was dressed in their Sunday finery. The third man, a lean, older gentleman with a shock of red hair, wore a mis-matched coat and trousers, his shirt tails hanging loose about his waist.

'What shall become of Morning Mass?' the man asked, plaintively.

'There may be some delay,' replied Bowman.

'Perhaps we need prayer this morning, more than ever,' opined Miss Bentley the organist.

Bowman nodded. 'Then we shall proceed as soon as we can.'

The crowd seemed satisfied at that. As the canon returned with several sheets of linen in which to wrap Milne, the men bent on the path to lift the body. As they did so, a button gaped open on his chest, exposing an area of flesh. Bowman gasped, his head suddenly swimming in confusion. There, standing proud from the man's pale skin, was a large blister. He had been branded with the mark of the Devil.

'The Kaiser?' Canon Tilcott's eyebrows rose high on his forehead. 'What on Earth can you mean?'

He sat with Bowman in the sacristy. It was a small, whitewashed room to the front of the chapel. The credens dominated the room. A large cabinet with wide but shallow drawers, it contained the vestments, altar dressings and hangings the clergy would use for their services. A small basin was set into the furthest wall, and a set of shelves was home to chalices and patens; small plates used to carry the Eucharistic bread to be consecrated during the Mass.

The inspector sighed. 'I was assigned to the docks at St. Saviour's,' he began, 'when I uncovered a plot to cause terror and panic throughout the Empire. The Kaiser was at its root.' He held up a hand to answer Tilcott's objection. 'The Kaiser's realm stretched from the docks to the West End. They extorted, bribed and murdered and held the city in their thrall. I had not thought to hear the name again.'

The canon shook his head. 'But I don't understand. Just how was Sartorius Milne connected?'

Bowman shifted uncomfortably in his chair, his palms sweating. The walls around him seemed suddenly to be closing in. 'The mark on his chest is a sign of ownership,' he said quietly. 'As one would brand cattle or a slave.' Tilcott tutted, sadly. 'It means he was the Kaiser's man.'

'I cannot believe it,' the canon was saying. 'Sartorius was a Holy man. Why would he find himself in such a predicament, in service to such a monster?'

'Desperation?' offered Bowman. 'Just how long had he been in service here at St. Mary's?'

'He joined us but recently,' the canon replied, his hands toying with the edges of his gown. 'Within the last two weeks. The previous sexton had succumbed to a fever and so I found myself in need of a temporary replacement. He came with excellent references so I had no hesitation in having him join us at St. Mary's.'

'Did you pursue his references?' Bowman asked, his moustache twitching.

There was a pause as the canon acquiesced. 'I did not.' Bowman raised his eyebrows. 'But what man does?'

Bowman sighed. 'What did you know of the man?'

'Only that he fulfilled his duties here to the letter.'

'What were his duties?' Bowman stood to stretch his

legs. A sudden groan from his stomach reminded him that he had yet to eat that morning.

'As sexton, his role was to support me in my ministrations. We are a small chapel as you have seen, inspector, so we have no need of a larger retinue. He was charged with the maintenance of the chapel and the cemetery on Prospect Place. That is all, but that is work enough.'

'Did you, in his time here, notice anything odd in Milne's behaviour?' Bowman was rubbing at his beard with a hand.

'Nothing at all,' the canon shook his head. 'He was the very model of the perfect sexton.'

There was a knock at the door and it swung open to admit the red-haired man in the creased shirt.

'Milne's body is at rest in the school rooms, Father,' he stuttered. 'A boy has been sent to the mortuary at New End.'

'Well done, Mr Thornicroft. Your help is much appreciated.'

'Do we know if he had any family at all, sir?' Thornicroft's eyes looked up balefully from behind heavy lids.

'We know next to nothing of the man,' Tilcott sighed. 'We can only hope that God will reward him for his service.'

Thornicroft nodded. 'Might we still have Morning Mass, Father?'

The canon stood to straighten his robes about him. 'Of course,' he replied with a nod of his head. 'Inspector, would you join us?'

St. Mary's Chapel had stood on the hill at Holly Place for the best part of eighty years, the first Catholic church to be built in Hampstead since the Reformation. The defeat of Napoleon had seen many French refugees return home to their native lands, leaving the chapel to serve a small community of worshippers. Its small but bright interior was flooded with light from arched windows that stood high in the chapel's vaulted ceiling. The nave was plainly decorated and furnished with hard, unforgiving pews. Wooden beams stretched across the ceiling and carvings depicting the life of Christ were placed at intervals around the walls. Statues of the Virgin Mary stood in alcoves, her arms held variously aloft to welcome sinners or at her breast to cradle her infant child. The sanctuary and side chapels were of a particularly opulent design. Bowman couldn't help but marvel at the intricacy of the detail. A lavish marble mosaic was pressed into the walls in the form of pillars and lintels to give the illusion of depth. Rich blues and deep reds were edged with a burnished gold. Doorways were framed with coloured tiles and a display of frescoes drew the eye up to the ornate ceiling. The overall impression was one of grandiosity and pomp, quite at odds with the meagre congregation that sat in the pews.

Bowman recognised them all as he followed the canon from the sacristy. Mr Thornicroft shuffled along to sit alone at the furthest wall from the aisle. Miss Bentley sat, her arms folded, with the man with the purple nose. His top hat lay on his lap, and Bowman could see him drumming his fingers upon it, expectantly. The lady in the green crinoline perched next to her husband, her eyes narrowing as the inspector made his way to a pew. She was clearly still not impressed with Bowman's demeanour. Other familiar faces he had last seen at the porch stared back at him; a governess, having seen her charges home, had returned to sit with a husband and wife. A couple of paupers had made their way through the open door to take their seats in the corner by the entrance. One gnawed on a crust of bread, while the other looked about in awe. Bowman took his place at the back of the chapel opposite the vagrants, intending to use the opportunity to observe the small congregation further.

Instead, much of the service passed Bowman by in a blur. The monotonous readings and proclamations from the altar served only to lull him into a state somewhere between asleep and awake. Indeed, by the time the bread and wine had been consecrated, he had felt his eyelids growing heavy. There was something about the quality of the canon's voice that he found particularly soporific. As he slipped into a netherworld of sleep, he was affronted with images of hooded figures, snapping jaws and deep, swirling water. Struggling for breath, he felt the water rise about him until it covered his mouth and nose. He looked wildly about him for any means of escape, but a hound held his leg tight in its jaws. He was helpless and bound to drown. In his struggle for air, Bowman let go a snort that jolted him awake. He looked guiltily around him. He was caught in the gaze of the woman in the green crinoline, and shuffled uncomfortably beneath her disapproving glare.

Looking to the front of the chapel, he saw the small congregation in the midst of Holy Communion. As Miss Bentley played the organ from the gallery behind, the motley members of the church queued to take the wafer and wine from Canon Tilcott. Perhaps eager for what little free wine could be had, even the vagrants were shuffling slowly forwards to their moment of salvation. The canon looked disapprovingly towards Bowman as the inspector scratched at the beard on his chin. As the congregation took their places for the final prayer, Bowman noticed Tilcott was standing in his place before the altar with no intention of moving. He raised his eyes to Bowman and gestured he step forth to take communion.

Bowman swallowed hard. As a committed rationalist, he found the ritual of transubstantiation strange. The literal belief that the wine and bread would turn to the blood and flesh of Christ was hard to credit. Could he stand before the altar in his current state? Looking around, he saw all eyes were upon him. Even Miss Bentley had paused at the organ. In the silence, Bowman found himself shuffling along his pew to the aisle. He cleared his throat and stepped towards the altar, the tapping of his shoes echoing from the tiled floor. His head was swimming. Once or twice he had to reach out to a nearby pew to retain his balance. The lady in the green crinoline was not impressed. Finally, he stood rather awkwardly before Father Tilcott. His eyes shone with a beatific light. There was a benevolent smile on his face. Bowman flinched instinctively as Tilcott reached out to him with the wafer.

'The body of Christ,' he said. Bowman blinked, suddenly uncomfortable. Tilcott raised his eyebrows, expectantly. Bowman's eyes flicked to the congregation. They sat in a sombre silence, each leaning forward to see the detective inspector take the sacrament. Bowman was chewing on his lip. His neck burned beneath his collar. He felt unworthy. Surely, he was undeserving of the flesh of Christ?

'The body of Christ,' the canon repeated softly, his smile fading.

Bowman swallowed hard, steeling himself as he opened his mouth to receive the wafer.

A commotion at the door interrupted the ceremony, and Bowman turned to see two men in black standing at the chapel entrance. Behind them stood the young lad who had woken Bowman that morning.

'Ackerley Perkins, New End Mortuary,' the taller of the men proclaimed. He had skin as white as any cadaver and delicate, almost ladylike hands. His companion was a surly youth with unkempt hair and heavy eyes. He was clearly unhappy in his work. 'I hear you have a body for us.' This last was said with more enthusiasm than Bowman thought seemly, but he was grateful for the interruption.

'You'll find him in the school rooms through the side chapel,' Tilcott responded, placing the paten to one side. 'If you will follow me.' Bowman breathed a sigh of relief as the two men strode purposefully up the aisle, eager to be about their business.

'I was called from worship at St. John's,' Perkins was complaining.

'Ah,' Tilcott paused mid-step as he led the men from the

nave. 'Then you will know Detective Inspector Bowman. He says he worships at St. John's.'

The two men turned as one to look the inspector up and down, blank looks upon their faces. 'Can't say as I do,' breathed Perkins. The canon raised his eyebrows, pointedly.

'It's a big church,' offered Bowman by way of explanation, his moustache twitching comically on his upper lip. His best recourse was to change the subject. 'You work upon a Sunday?'

Perkins narrowed his eyes. 'Death never was a respecter of the calendar, inspector.' There was almost a note of contempt in his voice. Once again, Perkins cast his eyes over the dishevelled man before him. 'There's many of us that are called to work all days of the week,' he continued. 'Is that not so, Father Tilcott?' Bowman felt he stood accused, but for what crime he could not fathom.

The canon gestured with his arm. 'Please, Mr Perkins, may I take you to the body?'

With a last, pointed look at Inspector Bowman, the two men were led from the chapel. Suddenly fearful that the congregation had witnessed the strange altercation, Bowman looked into the nave. He was relieved to see that the gathered worshippers had taken Perkins' arrival as a signal the service was over. The last of them was making their way through the entrance, shaking their heads sadly at all that had passed there that morning. Miss Bentley was descending from her organ in the gallery by way of some side stairs, lifting her skirts from her ankles as she negotiated the steps with care. For a moment, Bowman stood, still and quiet, gathering his thoughts. His cause of action was clear. He would accompany the body to the mortuary and oversee the autopsy. The area immediately about the chapel must be searched and doors knocked upon for witnesses. Men would be needed from the police station at Rosslyn Hill and word must be sent to Scotland Yard. Perhaps Sergeant Graves would see fit to join him. He smoothed his hair with a hand as he contemplated what a picture he would present to the young sergeant. Perhaps he should also go home and change.

'How odd!'

The exclamation served to interrupt his reverie. Turning into the chapel, he saw Miss Bentley leaning over a wooden box by the doors. She lifted her eyes to the inspector, her hands holding the lid of the box ajar.

'Inspector, would you call Father Tilcott?'

'Why?' asked Bowman as he made his way down the aisle towards her. 'What is the matter?'

As he got closer, he could see that she was breathing deeply, her chest rising and falling in her excitement. She wore a puzzled expression as she spoke. 'This is the collection box,' she explained. 'Ordinarily, one might find a few shillings in here after Morning Mass.' She had something in her hand, 'But, look!' Her eyes widened as she held her hands out to the inspector. Bowman could see notes of every denomination and in a large quantity. 'There must be hundreds of pounds here,' Miss Bentley concluded, a wide, uncomprehending smile spreading across her face. Bowman reached out to take the bundle of notes and noticed there was more left in the box. It might well have been a man's whole life savings, he mused.

'And you are sure it was not there before Mass?'

'I am certain of it. I set the box myself. Someone in the congregation must have left it here.' Miss Bentley was placing the notes carefully back in the box. 'We can do many good works with this sort of money.' With a breath to steel herself, the organist lifted the box from its stand and made her way up the aisle to the side chapel. 'Father Tilcott must be told of this,' she exclaimed, barely hiding the excitement in her voice.

Bowman's eye was caught by a movement behind the door. Leaning slightly to his right, he saw the boy who had run to his door that morning.

'What is your name, boy?' Bowman enquired, gently.

The boy stepped gingerly from the porch. 'Robert Tompkins, sir,' he whispered.

'You've had a busy day, Robert.'

'Yes, sir.' The boy allowed himself a smirk at the understatement.

Bowman leaned back on a pew, affecting as casual a manner as he could under the circumstances.

'Where do you live, Robert?'

'Dove Street.' Tompkins nodded through the door to the street. 'By the workhouse.'

'Do your mother and father not wonder where you are?'

'They care little for me,' said Tompkins, sadly. 'And even less on a Sunday. Father works at the market and values Sunday as his day of rest. Mother is ill and spends most her days in bed.'

Bowman leaned closer to the boy, affecting a

conspiratorial tone. 'Then how would you like to play detective for the day?'

Tompkins' eyes widened with excitement. 'Me, sir?'

'Yes, sir, you, sir!' Bowman laughed. He reached out to straighten the hat on the boy's head. 'Detective Sergeant Tompkins.' Ridiculously, the boy stood stiffly to attention. For a moment, Bowman thought he might salute.

'Reporting for duty, sir!' Tompkins chimed, his face beaming. If only all his sergeants were so punctilious, thought Bowman, wryly.

'Just how well do you know the congregation here at St. Mary's, Robert?'

The boy relaxed against the wall as he answered. 'I'd know them all by sight if not by name,' he replied. 'I don't have much to do with any of them.'

'Oh?' Bowman's interest was piqued.

'Got ideas above their station, most of 'em,' the boy sighed. 'Very 'holier than thou', if you get me meanin'.'

Bowman allowed himself a smile. 'Did you see the contents of the collection box from your place at the door?'

'I weren't spyin', if that's what you mean,' Robert blushed. 'But yes, I did.' His eyes shone with a mischievous light. 'Who do you suppose would have such money to give?'

'You know these people, Robert. Would any among them have such means?' Bowman lowered himself onto the pew and gestured the young lad to sit opposite the aisle. Robert took off his hat and scratched at his head as he thought.

'P'raps,' said Robert, slowly. 'I know some of 'em got

money enough. Not sure if they'd have quite so much to give away.'

Bowman nodded, thoughtfully. 'Precisely,' he said, almost to himself.

'Is it to do with that man's death, inspector?'

'I think it might be, Robert,' Bowman was musing, gnawing at his lip. 'It might well be.' Robert was looking suddenly uncomfortable. 'Did you know him?' the inspector enquired, gently.

Robert shifted his weight on his seat and looked around for fear of being observed.

'I followed him home one day after school,' he began. 'Just playing, like, to see if he spotted me.'

'Go on,' Bowman smiled again. He was enthralled by the boy's playful spirit.

'I was duckin' behind trees and walking on the other side of the road so I wasn't seen, running to keep behind passing carriages and the like.' Bowman leaned in. 'He lives in a room off Gayton Road, but not alone.' Robert seemed reluctant to go on. Bowman shifted towards him and raised his eyebrows in a gesture of gentle coaxing. The boy took a breath. 'There's little 'uns with him. Some younger than me.'

Bowman swallowed hard before he continued. 'His children?' he asked cautiously.

'Not his own, no. He sends them out,' Robert said hesitantly. 'To do his work.'

'His work?' Bowman's customary frown cut all the deeper into his forehead.

'They're small, so they can creep in places. Open

windows, holes in fences.'

'You've followed them, too?'

'Once or twice,' Robert admitted. 'And I've seen what they do. They're thieves and looters. Six or seven of 'em there are, and he sends them out every night.'

'These don't much sound like the actions of a Holy man,' Bowman mused.

'He's as Holy a man as I am, inspector,' chortled the boy.

The inspector considered the sexton again in the light of Robert's information. Sartorius Milne was clearly not the man he was thought to be.

Bowman was interrupted in his thoughts by a movement from the nave. Ackerley Perkins was strolling from the side chapel, his surly colleague in his wake.

'We are to carry the body to the Black Mariah,' he pronounced.

Glancing through the door, Bowman noticed for the first time the large, black carriage that stood outside on the road.

'Will you be joining us at the mortuary, inspector?' Perkins threw a disparaging glance in the inspector's direction. 'Or are you keen to catch up on your sleep?'

Bowman was again reminded of the picture he must be presenting. Pulling his jacket about himself and smoothing his moustache between a finger and thumb, Bowman tried hard not to break the man's gaze.

'I will be there in time,' the inspector drawled. 'I have some other matters to attend to in the meantime.'

Perkins gave a shrug as he walked from the chapel to the road, gesturing with his long fingers that his companion should open the doors at its rear.

Suddenly energised, Bowman sprang from his place on the pew. 'Robert,' he said quickly as he looked around him. 'Would you happen to know where each of the congregation lives?'

'Reckon so,' the lad nodded, 'Why?'

The Soldier's Daughter's Home stood behind the police station on Rosslyn Hill, giving Bowman the perfect opportunity to commandeer several men to search the grounds of St. Mary's Chapel for evidence relating to the murder of Sartorius Milne. With a team of four or five constables despatched to the chapel, the inspector followed his diminutive companion to the impressive red-brick building behind the police station. Successive programmes of building work had seen smart dwellings spring up in rows around the perimeter where once stood open fields. Founded at the conclusion of the Crimean War, it had been intended as a home for female children orphaned by the loss of their parents in the conflict. Prince Albert himself had opened the present building, which was now large enough to accommodate two hundred girls.

'You say one of the congregation is matron here?' Bowman asked as he loped to the door with Robert.

'Mrs Featherstone,' his companion replied. 'She was widowed in the Battle of Balaclava and has been here forever.'

Bowman smiled at how a period of forty years could seem such an age for a boy so young. A rather brisk young lady met them at the door and led them to the matron's office; a high-ceilinged, wood-panelled room with large windows that gave out over the grounds to the south of the building. Bowman could see livestock in pens and several young girls seated on milking stools.

'The cows are kept to assist the girls in their training for dairy work.' Bowman turned to see the short lady who had held the parasol at the chapel. 'They also do all the housework and keep the building in the condition you see it. They make and mend their own clothes, assist in the kitchen and do all the laundry.' Mrs Featherstone seemed all the more formidable in her own domain. Even Robert Tompkins slunk to the corner of the room, a bashful look upon his cherubic face.

'Most impressive, Mrs Featherstone,' Bowman murmured, turning his hat in his hands.

'You are investigating the murder of the sexton at the chapel?' Mrs Featherstone sat heavily in her chair behind a large, panelled desk.

'I am.'

'It is a most unfortunate business,' Mrs Featherstone leaned back with a sigh. 'Why should murder come to St. Mary's?'

Up close and under much calmer circumstances, Bowman had the time to appraise the woman before him. She was a wide-hipped woman of middle years, her wide face, Bowman imagined, a homely beacon to the girls in her charge. And yet, there was something about her girth that might suggest a latent power, perhaps strong enough to kill a man with such a force as Bowman had seen that morning.

'How well did you know Sartorius Milne, Mrs Featherstone?'

'Hardly at all,' Mrs Featherstone shrugged. 'I miss the previous sexton, Mr Lightbody. Now there was a gentleman.' Bowman noticed a twinkle in Mrs Featherstone's eye as she spoke. 'Always a kind word, and pious too.' She folded her arms neatly across her bosom.

'May I ask,' Bowman sat in the chair opposite, 'how much a matron of your standing might earn in such a place as this?' He couched his words deliberately in terms, keen not to impose.

Mrs Featherstone nodded in understanding. 'A matron may earn up to twenty pounds a year,' she said, her voice neutral. 'In such a place as this.' A wry smile played about her lips. 'Not much, perhaps, but then I want for nothing, you see?' She spread her arms wide as she spoke. 'Accommodation is provided. I am lucky enough to have rooms within the school house.'

Bowman thought back to the bundle of notes in the collection box at St. Mary's. There had been hundreds of pounds. He doubted Mrs Featherstone had ever seen such an amount.

'And where were you before chapel?'

'I was here, inspector, as always.'

'Why did you not attend church with the girls?'

'I never do.' Mrs Featherstone rested her hands on the table before her and adopted a posture that Bowman was sure she used with her more slow-witted children. 'I am a Roman Catholic, Inspector Bowman, and I have dispensation from the board to worship at St. Mary's. My family were among the refugees from the French Revolution who settled here and worshipped here. St. Mary's was established for just such people, and I feel them around me on the pews and at the altar during communion. It brings me much comfort.'

Bowman nodded, slowly. 'I assume there are those who could corroborate the facts?'

Mrs Featherstone looked slightly hurt as she replied. 'Certainly. Many of the staff and children would have seen me here until shortly before the mass at St. Mary's. It is but a short walk, inspector. I would certainly not have had the time to chase Sartorius Milne up the street and garrotte him with a wire. Nor would I have the inclination.' The matron sat back in her seat, her mouth drawn up into a tight, defiant bow.

Bowman fidgeted where he sat. 'And what do you know of the Kaiser?'

'The Kaiser?' Mrs Featherstone's wide face creased into an expression of incredulity. 'What on Earth should this have to do with the Kaiser?'

'Have you heard the term in any other context but that of the German Empire?'

Mrs Featherstone leaned in, bemused. 'Should I have done?'

Bowman held her gaze for a moment, then turned to the young boy in the corner. Robert Tompkins, clearly bored, was looking around him and out the window.

'Thank you, Mrs Featherstone,' said Bowman as he rose

from his chair to leave. 'We shall leave you to your duties.'

'Mr Thornicroft,' announced Tompkins as he marched down Belsize Avenue. 'I know him well enough.'

'And is he always dressed so singularly?' Bowman thought back to the ginger-headed man in the mismatched clothes and creased shirt.

'Just the opposite,' sniggered Tompkins. 'He's usually to be found in his best bib and tucker.' Bowman smiled at the phrase. Tompkins was proving to be an entertaining addition to proceedings. 'And he lives just here.'

The inspector turned to see a flight of black and white tiled steps ascending from the road to a wide, wooden door, painted a dusty blue. One of four adjoined townhouses, number Thirty-One Belsize Avenue was better kept than most. The tiles had been recently washed and the sashes and doorframe had the look of fresh paint about them. A large bay window gazed out across the road and onto the parkland beyond. Bowman sprang up the steps and knocked loudly at the door.

'You're sure he lives on the ground floor?'

Tompkins nodded vehemently. 'Seen him come and go many times.'

'Robert, just why do you follow these people?'

Tompkins shrugged, 'Got nothing else to do, have I?' he grinned. 'There's no fun to be had at home, so I walk the streets and dream.'

'Dream?' Bowman raised his eyes, quizzically.

Tompkins scuffed the pavement with his shoe as he explained. It was a gesture Bowman couldn't help but find endearing. 'I like to wonder what's going on behind all these doors. Who the people are, what they do. Sometimes I follow them.' He had a bashful look about him. 'Sometimes I pretend to be them. I copy their walk and try to think like them.' He looked up from beneath the peak of his cap, afraid to catch Bowman's eye. 'Makes me feel grown up, I 'spose.'

'Robert Tompkins,' began Bowman as he rapped at the door again, 'you will make a fine detective one day.'

Tompkins pulled himself up a little straighter at the compliment. 'Is there no answer?' asked the lad from the bottom of the steps.

Bowman shook his head. 'Let's go round the back.'

The garden was long and narrow but immaculate. Brightly coloured tulips bobbed and bent in their beds alongside peonies, irises and bluebells. A gravel path led to a sundial in the centre of the garden with a small but manicured lawn beyond. A yew hedge marked the perimeter, with tasteful statues placed at intervals in alcoves. The back of the house was, likewise, smart and fastidious. The sills were free of dust and debris and the path around the house newly swept. Not a leaf, petal or piece of gravel was out of place.

'Nice place,' whistled Tompkins. 'Tidy.'

'Yes. Odd, isn't it?' Bowman was banging on the back door, his face clouded in thought.

The lad swept his cap from his head and wiped his forehead with a sleeve. 'Is it?'

'I think it odd that a man so fastidious as to keep his house and garden so tidy and to be usually seen, as you say, in his 'best bib and tucker', should today attend chapel in a mismatched suit and soiled shirt.'

'Spose so,' agreed Tompkins. He bent to scoop a handful of gravel, then let the stones run out between his fingers and back onto the path. The sound pleased him.

'Just where have you followed Mr Thornicroft, Robert?'

The boy shrugged. 'All round Hampstead mainly. He gets the train to work in the week and again on Sundays after chapel.'

'Where does he go?'

Tompkins grinned. 'There you have me, inspector. I can't keep up with a train. Not with these little legs.'

Bowman leaned into the pair of French doors that looked into a garden room. Through the warp of the glass, he could see an elegant grand piano situated before an ornate fireplace. Tasteful pictures adorned the walls and fine and delicate ornaments stood upon the mantel. It was a room of cultivated taste much like, Bowman guessed, the man who lived in it. He peered in closer to look at a collection of photographs on the piano. They were formal poses presented in heavy silver frames. A beautiful young woman sat, demure and comely in one, whilst another showed the same woman with two men on her wedding day. One was clearly Mr Thornicroft.

'When was Mr Thornicroft widowed, Robert?'

'Before he moved to Hampstead.'

'And what happened to his wife?'

'Accident, they say.' Bowman's moustache twitched at the news. 'He's never got over it.'

'I should think not,' murmured Bowman. As he looked

closer at the pictures, he was interrupted in his thoughts by the boy at his elbow.

'The Hunnifords live just up the road,' Tompkins offered, helpfully. 'The woman in the green dress and her husband at the chapel.'

Bowman turned, pulling Tompkins' hat from his head and tousling his hair. 'Then that is where we must direct our feet.' Bowman tossed the cap back on to Tompkins' head with a grin and the two detectives rounded the corner from the garden onto Belsize Avenue.

'It's the inspector from the chapel!' The lady in the green crinoline stood back from the door, her face creasing into the look of distaste that Bowman had seen at St. Mary's that morning.

'What does he want?' came a man's voice from within.

Bowman swallowed hard and was suddenly keenly aware of his dishevelled state. If only he had found the time to shave, he thought. Rubbing his hand across his chin, he opened his mouth to respond, only to be interrupted by the scamp at his elbow.

'What do you think?' Tompkins asked of the woman, 'He wants to ask some questions about the murder.'

The lady was joined at the door by her husband. He was a tall man, with a pair of pince-nez balanced on his nose and a broadsheet newspaper in his hand. 'I was about to go through my stocks and shares,' he complained. 'Must we do this now?'

'It is a matter of the utmost urgency, Mr Hunniford,' Bowman said, emphatically, 'we are investigating a murder, after all.' He leaned in closer. 'It would not do to be seen to be obstructing the police in the course of their duties.' Hunniford's eyes fell to the boy on the steps beside the inspector. 'He is assisting me in my enquiries,' explained Bowman, none too convincingly. Tompkins gazed up with defiance.

Hunniford looked up and down the road as if fearful to be seen admitting a Scotland Yarder into his house, then stepped back into the hall. 'Perhaps we should go through to the library,' he harrumphed.

Bowman lowered his eyes under Mrs Hunniford's censorious gaze and sloped into the hall almost apologetically. Tompkins, emboldened by his morning as a Scotland Yard detective, was altogether more brazen and even had the temerity to offer the lady of the house his cap as he passed.

'This is most irregular, inspector,' Thomas Hunniford began as he led the duo into the large, gloomy library. Shelf after shelf of books lined the walls; copies of Gibbons' History of the Decline and Fall of the Roman Empire jostled for space amongst the works of Shakespeare and Milton. One wall in particular, Bowman noticed, was given over to volumes concerning the economies and financial systems of Europe. 'We have given our maid of all work the morning off, and so we are left to our own devices for luncheon. I am sure my wife would appreciate it if you could make this quick, so she might have adequate time to prepare.'

Bowman turned to see Mrs Hunniford wringing her hands by the door. 'We are to entertain some important people from the bank, inspector,' she said, looking Bowman up and down. 'I don't think it would do for them to see you here.'

Mr Hunniford was leaning against his desk by the window. Although there were chairs enough for all in the room, including Robert Tompkins, it was clearly not his wish that anyone be seated. Bowman was used to such tactics. Hunniford clearly thought it more likely the interview would be a brief one if it were conducted on their feet.

'It seems Sartorius Milne was a newcomer to the area,' Bowman began.

'That much is true,' concurred Hunniford, folding his newspaper neatly and placing it on the desk beside him. 'I barely knew him. He was generally a private man, although I gather he was diligent in the performing of his duties as sexton for Father Tilcott.'

'You know nothing of his previous life?' Bowman's eyes narrowed as he spoke.

'Why should we, inspector?' chimed Mrs Hunniford from the door. Bowman turned to face her. She carried herself at her full height, noticed Bowman, her haughty features seeming to sit in judgement upon those before her.

'I am merely trying to ascertain just who would want Mr Milne dead, Mrs Hunniford.'

'You think we would simply confess to such a thing?' Mrs Hunniford fixed Bowman with a steely gaze.

Mr Hunniford cleared his throat from his place at the desk. 'Don't mind my wife, inspector. She doesn't hold with Scotland Yard.'

'Nothing but a bunch of nosey do-gooders,' hissed the lady as she moved to join her husband. 'Forcing your way into people's homes of a Sunday in plain view.' She tutted. 'What will the neighbours think?'

Tompkins rolled his eyes as he flicked lazily through a book he had found on the shelf.

'Surely it is of the utmost importance that we catch Milne's killer,' pleaded Bowman. 'Before he strikes again?'

His words had the desired effect. Both Mr and Mrs Hunniford flinched at Bowman's assertion. 'Do you think that likely?' whimpered Mrs Hunniford, her hand suddenly flying to the pearls at her neck. Whether she was frightened or perversely thrilled at the thought, it was difficult to tell. Mr Hunniford took the pince-nez from his nose.

'Of course, inspector,' he began, sheepishly. 'We will help in any way we can.'

'What is your trade, Mr Hunniford?'

'Trade?' Hunniford's eyebrows rose with indignation at the word, 'I am a banker, sir. With no less an institution than Barrett's Bank. I find myself at Swiss Cottage five days of the week.'

'He gets the seven fifty five.'

All heads turned towards Robert Tompkins. He was seemingly immersed in a copy of Alfred, Lord Tennyson's verses, but not so immersed that he couldn't find the time to interrupt the conversation.

'What did you say, boy?' rasped Hunniford.

'He gets the seven fifty five from Finchley Road,' he repeated, simply. 'On the Metropolitan Line.'

Bowman did his best to suppress a smile. Hunniford cleared his throat. 'Your companion is quite the detective, isn't he?'

Snapping his book shut and replacing it on the shelf behind him, Tompkins beamed at the recognition of his talents.

'Do you think it wholly appropriate, Inspector Bowman,' interjected Mrs Hunniford from her husband's side, 'that one so young should be involved in such an investigation?'

'He is proving to be invaluable,' responded Bowman, causing the young lad to stand even taller.

Mrs Hunniford threw a look to her husband that Bowman recognised from the porch of the chapel. 'Perhaps things are worse at Scotland yard than the press would have us believe?' She slipped her arm around her husband's in a display of unity.

'And the press would have us believe it is bad enough,' concurred Mr Hunniford, haughtily.

'Mr Hunniford, might I ask your salary?' Bowman had decided not to tread quite so delicately as he had with Mrs Featherstone.

Hunniford's face flushed. 'Hang you for your impertinence,' he boomed with indignation. 'What the devil does that have to do with anything?'

'Mr Hunniford,' Bowman continued, the very picture of

quietude. 'Did you leave a contribution in the collecting box at St. Mary's Chapel this morning?'

'That,' seethed Hunniford, 'is between me and my conscience.'

'He ain't got enough to leave that sort of money.'

All eyes turned again to the lad at the book shelf. Tompkins stared back, innocently, his hands in his pockets.

'If you don't get that boy out of my library, inspector, than I will,' keened Mrs Hunniford, a shrill note to her voice.

'What do you mean, Robert?' Bowman said, softly.

'Didn't you notice his shoes as we walked in?'

Hunniford's jaw dropped open in wordless protest at the interruption.

'Get him out!' screamed Mrs Hunniford, her hands quivering at her stomach. 'I will not be so abused in my own home.'

'His sole's flappin'' Tompkins clarified. 'I noticed it in the hall. And have you seen the dust on these shelves?' Dramatically, Tompkins ran his finger along the nearest bookshelf. A film of dust collected on his finger. Pursing his lips, he blew it into the room and watched it fall to the threadbare rug at his feet. 'There's no way they've got a maid of all work. Or if they have, they need to sit her down and give her what for.' His demonstration ended, Tompkins chuckled to himself and leaned back against the bookcase.

Glancing down at Hunniford's feet, Bowman could indeed see his right shoe was in something of a poor condition. As he peered closer, he saw the cuffs of his shirt were threadbare too, and there was a tear in Mrs Hunniford's dress just below the elbow. Bowman cursed himself for missing such telling details. He rubbed his face with his hand and shook his head to clear it.

'A substantial sum of money was deposited in the collection box at St. Mary's shortly after Morning Mass this morning,' he explained, wearily.

'Just how much?' Mrs Hunniford was leaning in to hear.

'Several hundred pounds,' Bowman said, simply. 'Would you have such a sum to give, Mr Hunniford?'

There was a heavy silence in the room. Mrs Hunniford turned to her husband, a look of abject defeat in her eyes. Hunniford swallowed hard and lowered himself onto his chair at the desk. Taking a breath, he picked absently at the gold inlay on the tabletop.

'Truth be told, inspector,' he began, 'Business is not what is was.' Mrs Hunniford reached out to comfort her husband, her hand resting gently on his heaving shoulder. 'The bank has been failing and several of the board have resigned.' He looked up at the inspector with sad eyes. 'I have been left to steer it through insolvency. So you see, Inspector Bowman, I would not have the means to leave such a donation.'

The couple made a sorry picture at the window and Bowman felt his conscience pricked at their plight. 'Then, Mr Hunniford,' he began, quietly, 'I have taken up too much of your time.'

Mrs Hunniford led Bowman and his boy back through the hall to the front door. As the inspector turned to tip his hat on the steps, he saw Mr Hunniford standing forlorn by the library door.

'I do know one who would have such money,' he offered, cryptically.

'Go on,' the inspector implored.

Hunniford moved to join his wife at the front door. 'Only last week, a customer visited to withdraw his life's savings. I had thought he had heard the news and come to move his money to a safer institution, but,' he ran his fingers through his hair, 'Perhaps there was something more to it.'

'How much?' asked Bowman, a note of urgency in his voice.

'The sum was six hundred pounds.'

Tompkins whistled at the amount, his eyes wide in disbelief.

'And did you know the man?'

'I did, inspector.' Hunniford looked up the road again before continuing. 'I would not ordinarily divulge such delicate information, but I have known the man for several years. Indeed, I have helped and advised him in all matters financial since first he came to my bank.'

Bowman leaned in. 'His name, Mr Hunniford? Would you tell me his name that I might know the man?'

'You know him already, Inspector Bowman, for he was at St. Mary's Chapel this morning. Mr Thornicroft of Belsize Avenue.' Hunniford stood with his hands on his hips. 'I should say that it was almost certainly he that left the money in the box.'

Bowman strode back to number Thirty-One with a renewed urgency in his step, such that Tompkins had to run to keep up.

'I'm surprised you didn't notice,' he was saying as he fought to keep pace with the inspector. 'It was plain enough to me!'

Bowman was bounding up the tiled steps, raising a fist to bang on the door. 'I was distracted,' he blustered. Peering in at the bay window to his left, he could discern no movement from within. Turning to the road once more, he caught Tompkins leaning against the low wall, a thoughtful look upon his face.

'What is it, Robert?' asked Bowman as he joined him at the bottom of the steps.

'I was just thinking.'

'Oh, yes?'

'You don't look like much of an inspector.'

Tompkins was clearly feeling emboldened by the time they had spent together that morning.

'You're not exactly catching me at my best,' agreed Bowman as he looked down at his dishevelled clothes. He had dressed in haste, he remembered, but perhaps that didn't entirely excuse the fact that his cuffs were unfastened and his shirt buttons misaligned. One side of his braces had come undone and swung at his waist, leaving his trousers to hang at a particularly inelegant angle. The inspector blanched as he considered just what a picture he must have presented to the Hunnifords.

'Ain't you go no one to look after you?'

Bowman's moustache twitched. 'No, I haven't, Robert,' he said quietly.

'Shame,' said Robert with a smile. 'Still, you stick with me and you'll go far.'

With his fingers clasping his lapels, the young lad rounded the corner to the garden, clearly more pleased with himself than he had ever been. 'You'll be needin' to gain entry to the property, then,' he announced over his shoulder as he walked down the side of the house.

Bowman squeezed at the bridge of his nose and gave a sigh. He had a feeling the young boy had cut straight to the heart of the matter.

Joining Tompkins in the garden, he found him leaned up against the French doors, his nose pressed against the glass.

'What are we looking for?' he asked.

'Any sign as to why Mr Thornicroft would go the trouble of withdrawing his life savings to leave at St. Mary's,' Bowman thought aloud. 'And why he was dressed so slovenly.' Tompkins raised his eyebrows at his companion's own demeanour. 'You mentioned he was not usually dressed so unkempt of a Sunday.'

'That's true. He's a smart man, usually,' Tompkins agreed.

'It seems his appearance this morning was quite at odds with his usual fastidiousness.' Bowman cast his eye around the man's immaculate garden. Not a blade of grass was out of place, not a single weed grew in the neat beds.

Why had he presented himself so dishevelled at chapel? 'Now, we just have to find a way to get in,' he murmured.

'Your wish is my command!' Theatrically, Tompkins stepped away from the French doors to allow one of them to swing outwards into the garden.

Bowman stood, open-mouthed. 'How did you learn such a thing, Robert?'

'I told you,' the boy explained, darkly. 'I followed one of two of Milne's boys about their business. Picked up a trick or two.'

Bowman marvelled at the boy's ingenuity. 'Then be sure to keep such tricks to yourself in future.'

Tompkins stood to attention and gave the inspector a smart salute in response. Bowman sighed and made his way carefully through the door, calling as he went.

'Mr Thornicroft? This is the police! Are you home?' With no response forthcoming, Bowman gestured it was safe for Tompkins to follow him. As the boy headed through the room to the hall beyond, Bowman turned to look at the photographs on the piano by the fireplace. The first, a large, faded picture of a young woman with a parasol at the seaside might well have been a picture of the late Mrs Thornicroft, thought Bowman, a fact confirmed by the next photograph along. There stood the same woman alongside her new husband with another in a formal pose. Though clearly taken in a studio, drapes had been hung behind them, along with boughs of leaves and flowers to create a celebratory pastoral scene. Holding the picture to the light from the French doors, Bowman gasped as he recognised the third person in the photograph. There, behind the happy couple and dressed in a smart frock coat and cravat, stood Sartorius Milne. Bowman peered closer to confirm the man's identification. Both he and Mr Thornicroft looked younger by several years, but it was clearly the sexton from St. Mary's Chapel. Thornicroft must have thought well of the man, mused Bowman, to have had him included in his wedding photograph. Bowman noticed the picture was slightly misaligned, its top corner lifting away from the board behind it. Looking closer, he could see a lighter-coloured paper behind it. Turning the frame in his hands, he swung the clips to one side to release the board that held the paper and glass. Peeling the photograph away, he released another piece of paper that had been folded in two. Smoothing it on the piano, he saw it was a funeral card in remembrance of Mrs Florence Thornicroft, dated Thirteenth June, Eighteen Eighty Four. So she had died eight years previously. The card gave notice of her burial at Hatfield Road Cemetery, in the town of St. Albans. Bowman was about to call for Tompkins when he heard a shout from an adjoining room.

'Inspector Bowman, come quick!'

Suddenly alert, Bowman dropped the card where he stood and ran to the hall. Turning to his left, he found himself in a small kitchen. A large sink stood to one side and a small stove huddled close to a flue by the chimneybreast. On the floor by a Welsh dresser, Bowman saw Tompkins, his eyes wide. In his hands, he held a smart frock coat and trousers. Each was soaked in blood.

'How do you explain this, inspector?' Bowman could see Tompkins was shaking where he stood, clearly overcome with the drama of his discovery.

'It's all right, Robert, you can put them down.'

Tompkins lowered the garments to the floor and ran to Bowman's side. His eyes pricking with tears, he grabbed the inspector by the arm for comfort.

'He killed him, didn't he?' he asked, plaintively. 'Mr Thornicroft killed Sartorius Milne.'

'I think so, yes,' Bowman said, carefully. 'It would explain why he had to change his clothes this morning.'

Tompkins nodded, sadly. 'Thought so.'

'The question remains, where is Mr Thornicroft now?' He bent down on his haunches and wiped Tompkins' tears away with a thumb. 'Robert, you mentioned Thornicroft would catch a train after chapel each Sunday.'

Tompkins nodded, glad to have his mind turned to other matters. 'That's right,' he sniffed. 'The eleven thirteen from Finchley Road.'

'That is on the Midland Railway, is it not?'

'It is,' Tompkins confirmed. 'It goes to Borehamwood and St. Albans on its way to Leicester and Derby.' Bowman stared, impressed with the young man's knowledge. 'Study the timetables, don't I?' Tompkins smiled. 'Reckon I might see these places one day.'

Bowman clapped a hand on the lad's shoulder. 'That day has come, Robert.' The inspector stood and smoothed his coat about him. 'At what time will the next train leave for St. Albans?'

Hatfield Road Cemetery lay but a short cab journey to the east of St. Albans station. Surrounded by green

151

parkland and mature trees, it was indeed a worthy place to be laid to rest for all Eternity. Each grave was adorned with kerbsets containing planted flowers, coloured gravel and stones or statues raised to the memory of the deceased.

The journey had been uneventful enough, but for Tompkins' clear excitement at finally being allowed to travel on the railways. He had bounced in his seat opposite the inspector for almost the whole journey, thrilling as the train passed through each station or tunnel. Finally they had arrived at St. Alban's station, and caught a hansom to the cemetery. It was small enough that Bowman was sure they would see him. Sure enough, as they rounded the corner near the small chapel at its entrance, he saw the man leaning at a grave in a corner, shaded from the midday sun by a huge cedar tree.

'Mr Thornicroft?' Bowman offered as he approached.

The man looked up, his ginger hair flashing in the midday light. 'Ah, Inspector Bowman,' he nodded, resigned. 'I thought it was only a work of time before you found me.' Thornicroft stood, wiping his hands on his shabby trousers. He looked older to Bowman than he had that morning. 'The wonder is that it was so quick.'

'I had the best help a Scotland Yarder could wish for.' Bowman threw a look to his companion. Tompkins had decided to hang back, sensing the end of the adventure was near. Still, he was close enough to throw the inspector a delighted smile at the remark.

'You have come to arrest me, of course,' Thornicroft was saying, his hands resting in his pockets. 'For the murder of Sartorius Milne?'

Bowman nodded. 'Why was he at your wedding?'

Thornicroft looked at the inspector in surprise, then nodded in understanding. 'Of course,' he whispered. 'The photograph in the garden room. I trust you left the place as tidy as you found it?'

'We did,' said Bowman sharply. 'Save for the clothes in the kitchen.'

'Ah, yes.' Thornicroft lowered his eyes to his wife's grave. 'It was a messy business, I'm afraid. Florence would not have approved.'

Bowman was sure he could see the man's lower lip trembling. 'Did you know Milne had been in the Kaiser's employ?'

Thornicroft nodded, sadly. 'I followed the investigation in the papers, inspector. Certain details chimed deep within me, and I knew that Milne had fallen prey to just such a creature.'

'How did you know the man?'

Thornicroft looked up to the sky. A bank of cloud was moving in from the town. Perhaps there would be rain.

'We were raised as brothers.' Bowman's eyebrows shot up at the revelation. 'Sartorius Milne was adopted into my family as a young boy. I was only nine years old myself, but soon we were inseparable. We shared everything, inspector. Food, clothes and adventures. As we grew older, however, I found something I didn't want to share.' His eyes flicked down to the gravestone by his side. 'My dear Florence,' he sobbed. 'By the time I met my wife, Sartorius was a ne'er-do-well. Perhaps as a result of him being orphaned so young, he had become bitter and dissatisfied at his station in life. He turned to petty crime and drug addiction. He would disappear for days on end, only to be found in some pot-house.'

'And yet, you invited him to your wedding?'

'Only to appease my mother,' Thornicroft spat the words. 'It only served to heighten his dissatisfaction with life. To stand so near the object of his desire was painful.'

'Your wife?'

Thornicroft nodded. 'His desire was intense. It was all I could do to protect her from him. But my protection was not enough.' He was making fists with his hands in his anguish.

'He killed your wife?' Bowman heard Tompkins speak up from behind him. If Thornicroft thought it odd that an inspector should be accompanied by so young an accomplice, he did not show it.

'Some years after our marriage, Milne simply disappeared. In time I lowered my guard, and that's when he struck.'

'Why would he kill the woman if he loved her so?'

Thornicroft smiled sadly at the young lad's interjection. 'You are young and cannot understand the secrets of a damaged heart. Sometimes boy,' he continued, 'we hurt the thing we love. And if we love it entirely, we hurt it all the more.' Bowman swallowed as the man's words cut deep. 'So it was with Sartorius Milne.'

'Why did he never stand trial for the crime?'

'To my everlasting shame, inspector, I protected him.'

Tompkins was by Bowman's side now, clutching at his

arm once more. He glanced up with a sad look that only served to remind the inspector that, for all his bluster and bravado, he was no more than a child.

'I had left Florence alone to travel to the south coast. I have an interest in the bones that have been found in the rocks at Lyme Regis. They are thought to be the remains of fantastical beasts. Whilst there, I received word from Sartorius himself that he had killed my wife. He put it in a telegram, no less.'

'Why didn't you turn him in?' Tompkins was agog at the story.

'He was my brother!' cried Thornicroft. 'I took the first train home and found her where he had left her. We lived on a farm in the open country near St. Albans in those days, and it was a simple matter to move her to a barn where we stored a mechanical thresher. It was even more simple a matter to let the thing topple upon her, as if her death had been an accident.' Thornicroft's hands were at his face, rubbing furiously at the tears that coursed from his eyes. 'I regretted it at once of course, but now I was complicit.'

'And when did you move to Hampstead?'

'Some five years ago, to put the matter behind me.' Thornicroft dropped to his knees at his wife's graveside. 'Of course, I could not. I hope you never feel the ravages of grief, inspector.'

Bowman swallowed hard, his neck burning beneath his collar. He was engulfed with a sudden cold sweat. 'I have felt them already,' he said, quietly. Looking down to his companion, he saw Tompkins staring back, his face the very picture of cherubic innocence.

'Then you will know how it burns at the soul,' Thornicroft gasped. 'Until it cannot be called a soul at all.'

Bowman's mouth had dried. 'Milne had fallen foul of the devil in the dock,' he rasped, swallowing again. 'When the Kaiser was defeated, he must have fled the docks in search of a new life.' Bowman was piecing the events together in his mind as he spoke. 'And so he came to Hampstead.'

'I saw him, inspector, in Holly Place one day, in his sexton's garb.' Thornicroft was breathing heavily in remembrance of the event. 'I declined to go to chapel for the first week, but instead looked into his activities. I found him living in rooms with children and using them for his own ends. I did not wish to know to what extent. But I knew from the start, that I must kill him.'

'Why did you not come to the police?'

'To have him slip through my hands again? I could not face it, inspector.' Thornicroft was shaking now. 'Thus far, I had lived my life without sin.' His eyes flicked to the chapel at the entrance to the cemetery. 'But I knew I would be damned by my actions. To atone for my transgression, I determined to leave my entire life's savings to the chapel.'

'Mr Hunniford said as much,' Bowman said, though he was not sure the man was listening.

'I took the wire from my garden and followed him to the chapel this morning,' Thornicroft continued. 'He opens the doors early to carry out his duties, so I knew I would not be seen. Besides, I was quick. As he turned back to the chapel door and fumbled for the keys, I struck. In that moment, inspector, I had the strength of ten men, and I squeezed.' Tompkins buried his face deeper into Bowman's sleeve as the man spoke. 'And then I rushed home to change. In my haste to kill the man, I had not considered there would be so much blood.' Thornicroft clawed at his coat as if the blood still dripped there. 'I could not be seen to be late, lest suspicion fall upon me, and so I took whatever clothes I could find. I took my money for the collection box and attended chapel for the last time.'

Bowman's moustache twitched at his upper lip. 'The last time?' he queried.

There was a flash of light as Thornicroft pulled a blade from his pocket.

'No!' screamed Tompkins as he rushed from Bowman's side. Jumping high, he caught Thornicroft by surprise, and the man lowered the blade from his throat. Tompkins was hanging from his arm now, and Thornicroft tried to shake him off.

'Let me go, boy! I must be with Florence!'

Bowman lurched forward to force the man's arm up behind his back. With a yelp of pain, he let go the knife and Tompkins ran to retrieve it.

'Let me die, inspector,' Thornicroft cried. 'It is no less than I deserve.'

'You will be with Florence soon enough, Thornicroft,' Bowman soothed. 'But not today.'

The Silver Cross was the perfect place to introduce

Tompkins to his first beef and ale pie. Bowman sat across from him at the table, in his favourite chair by the fire. He had been amazed by the young lad's resilience and resourcefulness throughout the course of the investigation, and thought the least he could do was treat him to a decent meal. He had ignored Harris the landlord's questioning look and ordered a pint of porter for himself and a pie for the boy. The inspector chuckled as he saw with what haste the boy was devouring his supper.

'When's our next case, inspector?' Tompkins grinned as he wiped gravy from his mouth with a sleeve.

'Rest assured I shall call upon you when I have need,' returned Bowman, lifting his glass to his lips. The porter was rich and malty and quenched his thirst admirably. He might even stay for a few more once Tompkins was on his way.

'Do you always need so much help?' the lad asked, a mischievous gleam in his eye.

Bowman thought for a moment of Sergeant Graves. Tompkins had more than made up for his absence during the case, but he was eager to make his acquaintance again.

'We all need a little help sometimes, Robert.'

'I shall remember that,' said Tompkins through a burp. 'When I am a real detective sergeant.'

~

THE HOLBORN STRANGLER

JUNE, 1892

The Silver Cross was busy. As Detective Inspector
George Bowman sat in his favourite chair by the fireplace,
he let his eyes wander over the eclectic clientele that
clamoured for attention at the bar. Three or four labourers
had forsaken their work and started their drinking duties
early. They raised tankards of Harris' best foaming ale and
toasted each others' health before downing the contents in
one draft, smacking their lips as the dregs dripped from
their beards and moustaches to the floor. A businessman,
resplendent in his silk top hat and fur-trimmed frock coat,
sipped daintily at a glass of port, his keen eyes scanning
the saloon for any who might recognise him. All the talk
was of the escaped murderer, Hubert Kabble. A fugitive
since his escape from the black maria on his way to his
hanging at Newgate, Kabble was known to be ruthless and
violent. The crime for which he had been condemned had
been particularly heinous; the killing of a young woman
known to be his betrothed during an argument over his
drinking habits. His reputation had been sealed by the
resultant murder of the two policemen who had
accompanied him on his ride to the gallows. Kabble had
hidden a razor blade beneath his tongue, with which he had
despatched the two young officers the moment the doors
were opened. Investigations were now under way to
determine just how he had effected his escape from the

prison grounds so easily.

Bowman rolled his eyes as a young man in a bowler hat and tattered waistcoat took his place at the piano stool. If he had been sober he might have been proficient enough, mused the inspector as he sipped at his porter. As it was, the young man attempted to ascend the heights of Abdul Abulbul Amir with shameless abandon, but reached only the foothills of mediocrity, such was his lack of talent. Bowman winced as whole chords were mangled and the tune drifted off into unknown territory. Several of the heaving crowd attempted to sing along, but all were thwarted by the vagaries of the melody. They seemed to shrug as one as the young man gave in to his drunken state and let his fingers wander aimlessly up and down the keyboard in lieu of a tune. Amidst the melee, Bowman caught the landlord's eye and raised his almost empty jar in his direction. With a nod of understanding, Harris sent his boy to the table with another draught of porter. 'This is for the inspector,' Bowman heard him say above the hubbub. 'But tell him it's his last.' The inspector swallowed at the implication and felt a blush come to his cheeks. Stroking his moustache between his thumb and forefinger, he wondered quite how long he'd been sat at his table. He cast a lazy eye through the window to Whitehall beyond, and could see it was flooded with a golden, morning light. Passersby sweated their way to their destinations, their tempers rising with the temperature. Bowman saw several children sitting on the kerb, their bare legs stretched out into the road, heedless of the rattling carriages that passed just inches from their shoeless feet. A street trader tried in vain to sell sausages of questionable heritage from a pan sizzling at a brazier. Every now and then, a police constable would pass the window on his beat, causing Bowman to sink even lower in his chair for fear of discovery. A detective inspector's life was meant to be a busy one and Bowman was in no doubt that questions would be asked if he was discovered having spent the best part of the day in The Silver Cross. They were questions that Bowman hardly dare ask himself and if he did, he wasn't entirely sure he'd have the answers. All he knew was that, in recent days, he had found more comfort in the bottom of a glass than in anything else. More importantly, he had noticed with growing despair, the increase in consumption of his favourite porter had coincided with the diminishing of the dreams that had plagued him. All he had to do now, was hide it from his colleagues. Bowman knew he would have to be careful. Inspector Ignatius Hicks had it in for him. The bluff inspector had complained to the commissioner himself of Bowman's erratic behaviour. Every word from Bowman's mouth, every look and gesture was now subject to the utmost scrutiny. It was Sergeant Graves that Bowman felt sorry for. Up until very recently, Bowman had considered himself something of a mentor for the young sergeant. Now, he considered himself a liability. He felt he had let Graves down.

Bowman looked up sadly as Harris' boy placed his next glass of porter on the table. Holding out his hand for payment, the lad fixed Bowman in his gaze. The inspector shifted uncomfortably in his seat as he reached into his pocket for some change.

'You don't look like an inspector,' asserted the boy, bravely.

Bowman's jaw hung slack. Unsure what to say, he merely dropped a few coins into the boy's hand and waved him away. Bowman swallowed again and looked about him, in dread that the boy's announcement had been overheard. The labourers were raising another round of drinks to each other, the businessman was nodding to sleep over his copy of the Evening Standard. Bowman pulled himself up in his seat and straightened the tie around his neck. Clearing his throat, he eyed the freshly delivered pint of porter before him. Harris was right. This would be his last one, the inspector told himself, and he would be on his way. He had barely had the time to reach for his jar, however, when the door was thrown open to admit a tall, young man with a mop of curly, blond hair. Sergeant Anthony Graves was dressed in heavy corduroy trousers and a bottle-green velvet waistcoat with shining silver buttons. His jacket was slung over his shoulder as he panted in the doorway, his eyes falling exactly where he had thought to see his superior. 'Sir,' he began, panting. 'You're to come quickly.'

'What is the matter?' Bowman asked, his eyes flicking guiltily to the glass in his hand.

'Hicks is up to his eyeballs in a matter,' Graves huffed, his face flushed from the summer heat. 'I think it best you come at once. There's been another one.'

'Another what?' Though tall himself, Bowman was

struggling to keep up as Graves' long legs carried him through Trafalgar Square to St. Martin's Lane. 'And where are we going?'

'Holborn, sir,' said Graves, simply. 'There's been another strangling.' To Bowman's evident relief, Graves slowed his pace outside a horse market on Upper St. Martin's Lane and hailed a cab at the roadside.

'I'm not for hire for so quick a journey,' the driver was complaining from his perch, 'Holborn is but a walk away.' Even his horse had a haughty look about him, marked Bowman, seeming to look down his long muzzle at the two sweating detectives.

Graves drew his identification from his pocket. 'This is police business,' he asserted as he unfolded the paper beneath the man's eyes. 'You will take us where we please, and for now that is Old Bell Yard.' The two Scotland Yarders climbed aboard as the driver rolled his eyes in resignation. He cracked his whip at the mare in her harness, muttering something under his breath that Bowman couldn't quite hear. The horse moved reluctantly into the middle of the road and before long, was trotting at a pace through Castle Street. Bowman drew deep on the sweet smell of hops that emanated from the brewery belching steam into the air as they passed.

Graves turned to his superior, a look of triumph on his face. Flashing the inspector a grin, he settled back in his seat and tucked his papers back inside his jacket pocket. 'Perks of the job,' he winked.

As ever, Bowman envied his companion's cheery disposition. Even in the face of the most dire circumstances, he seemed always to be ready with a smile or a quip. In the hands of others such gestures might seem facile, but Graves seemed to exude such an air of innocent enthusiasm that they were eminently forgivable.

'Inspector Hicks is in a pickle,' Graves elucidated as they rattled through the streets. 'He's been charged with the investigation of two murders over the past few days.'

'Two?' Bowman's eyebrows rose at the thought.

Graves nodded, almost enthusiastically. 'The latest, a young woman, was found near Holborn Viaduct in the early hours.'

Bowman clutched at the side of the carriage as the hansom navigated a particularly rough patch of road. 'Both strangled?'

'Without a doubt,' confirmed Graves, his eyes bright.

'And are they connected in any way?' Bowman was thinking hard, grateful that his head was clearing in the open air.

Graves leant across to the inspector, warming to his theme. 'They were each discovered early in the morning,' he began. 'In thoroughfares off the main roads.'

'This is all as you might expect,' ventured Bowman. 'To strangle someone on the main roads would be to risk discovery or disturbance. Does Hicks believe it to be the work of one perpetrator?'

'Inspector Hicks is at a loss.' Graves was clearly deriving much pleasure from the telling of his story. 'I have repeatedly suggested that we call upon you but he has resisted until now.'

'Why has he waited so long to call me in?'

The silence was deafening. Graves' open face was always an easy one to read. Right now, it spoke volumes. It was there in the way Graves averted his eyes and in the uncharacteristic frown upon his forehead. The meaning was clear, even in the sergeant's reticence to speak. Hicks did not trust him. Bowman shook his head in exasperation and settled back in his seat to endure the journey.

The carriage clattered between the tightly packed buildings on Parker Street before veering wildly onto Little Queen Street and then east onto High Holborn. An eclectic jumble of buildings flashed past. The Novelty Theatre threw open its doors to admit the early matinee audience, a motley ragtag of street dwellers eager to escape the heat amid the seedy looking gentlemen in tattered clothes, faded hats and scuffed shoes. The vista opened up as they drove on, and Lincoln's Inn Fields revealed itself in the morning sun. The trees wore their full coats of luscious green and the hydrangeas displayed their blowsy blooms with pride. Children ran among the beds of lavender, pursued by a particularly excitable dog with a stick between its teeth. Squeezing through an alley so tight that Bowman felt he should breathe in to fit through, the hansom careered onto High Holborn at some pace. As ever, the inspector was struck by the strange juxtaposition of ramshackle buildings and grander edifices. He noticed tall, Palladian columns standing to attention at the entrance to a bank whilst, next door, a butcher's shop stood at a haphazard angle, leaning with relief against the bulwark of its sturdier neighbour. The driver navigated the oncoming traffic with great skill. He was clearly eager to be at his destination as soon as possible, the quicker to return to his stand, there to await a paid fare. He swerved through the throng of milling pedestrians with elan. Traders and hawkers were in full cry, their melodies mingling with the melee of shouts and calls that rose from the pavements. At this hour, the shops were full. Provisions for the day were purchased. A line of shop workers snaked from a baker's stall, all eager for a pie. A public house threw open its doors to all manner of custom, from the smart businessman looking for a quiet nook in which to peruse his copy of The Times to the gaggle of powdered women eager to spend their night's earnings. A line of smart carriages awaited their turn outside the First Avenue Hotel, the drivers leaping from their perches to open their doors to elegant women in summer dresses.

The road grew wider still the further east they travelled. Here, the traffic was so heavy that the street could barely be seen beneath the clattering wheels and stamping hooves. Not an inch of space was clear for a moment before it was filled with a scrum of horse and carriage. They ranged in size from the single pony trap to the grand brougham, each stirring the filth from the road as they churned their way to their destinations. The smell of sweat rose from the horses, assailing Bowman's nostrils as he wiped the dust from his eyes. Ahead of them, a statue to Prince Albert himself sat astride his horse at Holborn Circus, flanked with figures in brass representing peace and commerce, his hat raised in cheerful greeting. Though some of the most successful companies were headquartered along the five streets that crossed the circus, it was a district of mixed fortunes. Neither far enough west for the smarter shops nor far enough east to catch business from the city, it struck an unhappy medium between prosperity and degradation. Even at this hour, several drunks were leaning for support against the statue and, looking to his left down Leather Lane, Bowman saw a fight in progress between three scruffy labourers as they passed. Just before climbing the height of Holborn Viaduct, the carriage slowed at the turning to Old Bell Yard.

Detective Inspector Ignatius Hicks was difficult to miss. As soon as the carriage pulled up at the roadside, Bowman spotted him. Even in the heat of the late morning, he was dressed in a heavy coat, his great, unruly beard spreading out across his barrel chest and shoulders as if it were a creature yet to be tamed. He spread his arms wide as he attempted to control the crowds that had gathered, marshalling them this way and that as they attempted to go about their business of the day. The crowds made way as Bowman and Graves alighted their cab, the driver snapping his whip with a haughty harrumph at his lack of payment. As the hansom turned in the road and rattled off to Broad Street, the throng spilled into its wake so that soon it could not be seen through the mass of bodies and bobbing heads.

Even here, Bowman could see the Holborn Viaduct rearing above them and over Farringdon Street like a colossus. Linking Holborn with Newgate Street and the

City of London's financial district, it was opened by Queen Victoria herself and provided a level approach into the City. Bowman just about remembered a time when progress over the valley necessitated a long ride along Charterhouse Street to Holborn Bridge, there to cross the River Fleet to Snow Hill. Progress was a remarkable thing, he mused, but as ever it advantaged only those with money in their pocket. The way to the City had been opened up for financiers and bankers but that was little in the way of comfort to Holborn's poorer citizens. At least, thought Bowman wryly, they got to shelter beneath the huge arches that spanned the roads.

There is nothing more that the inhabitants of London enjoy, noted the inspector as he strode towards Hicks, than a spectacle, the grislier the better. It brought a little colour to their drab lives. Death was a neighbour to many in Holborn and his work commonplace. The crowd exhibited no great surprise at this latest display of his handiwork, but rather stood in awe and spoke in hushed tones of reverence.

'They've found another,' Bowman heard an old crone whisper to her companion. She had a face as lined as some of the dried fruit Bowman could see in her hand, and a sore on her neck. 'E's struck again,' she said with evident relish, her words greeted with furious nods and murmurs of agreement from those around her.

'Ah, Bowman!' boomed Hicks, blinking sweat from his eyes. 'I do hope we didn't tear you from your morning ablutions.' The insinuation was clear in the tone of his voice as he folded his arms across his chest. Clamping his teeth around the bit of his pipe, he raised his eyebrows in expectation of a response. Bowman looked around at the assembled crowd. The last thing he wanted was to become a public entertainment.

'What do we have, Hicks?' asked Bowman, meeting his fellow inspector's gaze.

'If you had but read the papers,' Hicks puffed, 'you might well have hazarded a guess of your own.'

With a start, Bowman realised he had no idea what day it was. It seemed but a few days since he had investigated the murder of Sartorius Milne at Hampstead, but he couldn't be entirely sure. He had barely felt the sun on his face since, let alone read the papers. With a pang of guilt, his mind flashed back to his rooms in Belsize Crescent and the battered chaise longue upon which he had passed many recent hours. He remembered the days that had passed in a fog of Madeira and gin. Shaking his head to clear the image for fear it would be read in his face, Bowman cleared his throat.

'I have been otherwise engaged,' he stammered, defensively.

'Then you will not have heard of the other murder!' The shout came from the crowd and Bowman turned to see a rangy youth with a tray of bread, come to ply his trade amongst the crowd.

'How could he not have heard?' questioned another. 'The talk has been of little else!' Bowman met the eye of a man in an old fashioned frock coat with a wide collar. 'Unless we know more than Scotland Yard!' The crowd jeered at this and Bowman noted the looks of suspicion in their faces.

'Be on your way!' Hicks boomed, gesturing with a wave of his hand that the crowd should disperse. In response, one or two amongst the throng shuffled away, only to find another vantage point from which to view proceedings. Most showed no intention to budge at all.

Bowman turned to Graves, furrowing his brow. 'What have I missed, Graves?'

'A man found yesterday morning, just three streets away,' the sergeant began. 'Same as the girl this morning. No sign of a robbery,' he continued, in answer to the inspector's unspoken question. Graves led the inspector further into the alley and away from the main road. Hicks accompanied them, burying his hands deep in his pockets as if in a sulk.

'It was Graves' idea to call you in,' he thundered. 'I'd have got to the bottom of it meself given time.'

'How long have you been with the body, Inspector Hicks?' Bowman threw the words over his shoulder like scraps to a dog.

'Since eight of the clock,' Hicks said, pointedly.

'And what progress have you made in the investigation?'

Hicks huffed as he struggled to keep up.

'He has made none,' began Graves, gleefully. 'And has finally relented to my suggestion of bringing in a fresh pair of eyes.'

The young lady lay spread-eagled on the alley floor. A basket of lavender had been spilled amongst the filth and a few coins glinted in the sun. An unsmoked cheroot lay discarded on the ground some feet away.

'They didn't even stop to pick up her change,' mused Bowman as he squatted on his haunches. 'As you say, Graves, hardly the marks of a robbery.' Graves nodded silently. 'There is no sign of her having been defiled?' It seemed the woman had remained fully clothed throughout her ordeal.

'Not to my knowledge,' Hicks coughed into his sleeve.

Bowman's eyes rose up the unfortunate wretch's body. Her tattered coat had slipped from her shoulder to reveal an even tattier dress, the buttons of which remained fastened across her body. Peering closer, Bowman could see bruising about her neck. The skin had been punctured in several places; an indication of the force employed to silence the girl. Bowman breathed deep to settle his stomach.

'Was it the same with yesterday's victim?'

Graves nodded. 'Exactly the same,' he confirmed.

Bowman rose to his feet, shaking his head at the depravity of it all. 'Have you made any attempt to identify her?'

'I have barely had the time,' Hicks protested. 'But I have sent Constables Roach and Baker out onto the streets with her description. She is a flower seller. If this is her usual patch, she must be known in the area.' He placed his hands on his wide hips, puffing out his chest with the certainty of his pronouncements. 'I doubt an identification will be long.'

Bowman frowned in consternation. What could possibly be the motive for such a crime? The evidence suggested it was certainly not robbery and he was content to take Hicks' word that the body had not been defiled. It seemed the murderer had simply strangled the poor lady for no apparent reason, then gone about his business. That fact alone troubled Bowman considerably. Turning to the alley's entrance he saw an ambulance pulling to a halt, its driver leaping from his perch to retrieve the stretcher from its rear doors.

'I'm having the body sent to Doctor Crane at Charing Cross,' Hicks clarified. Bowman nodded, unsure whether the good doctor would find much of use beyond the unfortunate woman's bruised neck.

'And the man you found yesterday?' Bowman rubbed his face with his hand. His skin felt numb.

'Now, there,' boomed Hicks, triumphantly, 'we've had rather more success.'

'Are you sure this is the place?' Bowman found himself standing before a ramshackle building off Lamb's Conduit Passage. Its greasy walls towered four storeys above him. In truth, he was grateful for its shade. Graves had marched him up High Holborn at quite a pace and, as they passed the many dingy chophouses and pie shops that stood on the roadside, Bowman realised that he had yet to eat a thing. His stomach growled in protest as they turned again off the main road. The crowds were thinner here, but still they had to weave between the detritus and debris that littered the ground as they picked their way towards their destination. More than once Graves called out a cheery greeting to a passerby, seemingly unconcerned whether they responded or not. Not for the first time, Bowman marvelled at his companion's irrepressible spirit. The sergeant was in his element when there was work to be done and, in the light of the morning's discovery, there was work aplenty.

'Certain of it,' Graves beamed. 'His name was Alfred Makin and he lived here at number three Lamb's Conduit Passage.'

'How can you be sure?'

Graves leant a shoulder against the wall, heedless of the mark it would leave, or the rat that scuttled between his feet. 'There were old injuries about him that reminded me of my father.' Bowman raised his eyebrows in surprise. He had never before heard Graves talk of his family. 'He fought with General Gordon in Khartoum.' Bowman noticed a far away look in his eye. 'He wouldn't talk much about it, but he came home bearing scars.' Graves scuffed the dirt on the street with his shoe. 'Above and beyond the heat and the dust and the diseases they fell prey to, the men were issued with malfunctioning weapons.' Bowman's eyes narrowed. He remembered the controversy over the fall of Khartoum at the hands of Mahdist rebels and had a vague memory of the press coverage. General Gordon himself had been slain and decapitated, his body supposedly dumped into The Nile. The fighting had been bitter, and Bowman could quite understand why Graves' father might never have spoken of it. 'My father was equipped with a Martini-Henry. They were usually reliable enough, but a consignment with a faulty cartridge chamber had been rushed to the battlefield.' Bowman had never seen his companion with so serious a look in his eye. 'When the chamber exploded, he was invalided home with injuries to his right eye and face. The same injuries were displayed by Alfred Makin, so I knew he was a military man,' Graves sighed. 'Might even have fought with my own father.' He walked to the other side of the street, raising his gaze to the home of the erstwhile soldier. 'At any rate, I thought I'd try my luck at The Viaduct Tavern.'

'The gin palace?' Bowman knew the establishment by reputation only. It stood opposite Newgate Gaol, just a few hundred yards from where he had spent the past hour at Old Bell Yard. Graves nodded.

'It has rooms for rent at favourable terms to old and injured servicemen, and there's many a customer that will stand an old soldier a pint or two. My father would spend an evening there when he felt the urge and I guessed Makin might, too.' Graves scratched absently at his neck. 'Turns out he spent his last evening there. They were pleased not only to furnish me with the poor man's name, but his address, too.'

Bowman looked with fresh eyes at the filthy tenement walls that rose before him. The filth-stained brickwork crumbled at his touch and he could see the glassless windows were framed with rotting wood. The makeshift doors could have afforded little security and Bowman shuddered to think of the life the old soldier must have led. Even in these sunny days, the alley stood in almost complete shade rendering the interior rooms, Bowman imagined, cold, damp and inhospitable.

'Poor recompense for the service he gave,' the inspector

muttered, struck by the fact that Makin had returned from one life of disease and hardship only to be rewarded with another. 'Did he have employment?' Bowman asked sadly.

'Intermittently,' replied Graves, quietly. 'By all accounts he found occasional work as a market porter.'

'Where was he found?'

'Not far from our lady in Old Bell Yard,' the young sergeant replied. 'Same side of High Holborn there's a passage called Furnival's Inn. He was discovered there in the same state. Nothing stolen.'

'Strangled?' Bowman's frown had returned.

'Strangled,' Graves dipped his head.

'Perhaps on his way home from The Viaduct?'

'It's a possibility.'

'Graves,' Bowman was rubbing his chin in thought, 'Have Hicks meet me at my office.' The young sergeant made as if to move. 'And Graves?' He turned to face the inspector. 'We really need a name for that poor young lady.'

Graves nodded. 'I'll see we get it, sir.'

Scotland Yard was in disarray. The news of Hubert Kabble's absconding from Newgate had provided Fleet Street with much needed copy over the previous week, and the Yard with a problem it could ill afford. Confidence in the Metropolitan Police Force seemed to ebb and flow with the Thames tide, but it appeared it had never been lower. Behind his desk, Sergeant Matthews was assailed on all sides. He recognised several reporters from The

Evening Standard, each of them eager to get to the heart of the story. In truth, there was little to tell. Kabble had simply taken his guards by surprise. A slight, sickly-looking man, he had been deemed a low risk by the authorities and so had been accompanied by a single guard. The black maria had driven at a stately pace through the gates to Newgate Gaol, where Kabble was to keep his appointment with the noose. As it rolled to a halt and the doors were opened by another, seemingly distracted guard, Kabble had slipped a razor blade from beneath his tongue and slit the throats of the two watchmen. Even as they gasped for breath, each grasping in vain at their necks, he had jumped from the carriage and slipped through the still-closing gates into the streets of Holborn beyond. An immediate search had been instigated but to no avail.

'Was the Yard at fault?' leered a particularly persistent reporter, the stub of a pencil poised at his notebook.

'It is not within Scotland Yard's purview to provide guards for prison transport,' sighed Matthews, his cherubic face flushing with the pressure of the interrogation.

'But it is within your purview to find him,' jeered another.

'And we are diverting all possible resources to just such an end.' The desk sergeant was making notes of his own in the ledger before him. Even in the midst of chaos, he had work to do.

'In the meantime, there's a killer on the loose. Should we be afraid?'

Matthews took a breath and launched into his prepared

response for what seemed the twentieth time in as many minutes. 'We would always urge the citizens of London to go about their business with caution.'

'So Scotland Yard can do no more than advise?' A barrage of laughter burst from the assembled crowd. Matthews looked up from his ledger to be confronted with insinuating looks and sly glances. Looking around the large reception hall, he saw that even the drunks on the benches beneath the window were giving him their undivided attention. Several ladies had broken their stride to hear his response, their hands flying to the pearls around their necks as if in a reflex reaction. Everyone, it seemed, lived in fear of Hubert Kabble.

'If you would excuse me,' Matthews blustered as he snapped the ledger shut. 'I have much to do.' Ducking from the desk, he stepped nimbly between the witnesses, police constables and felons who stood awaiting their fate.

'I knew Kabble!' The cry came from a gnarled looking man with a crooked back who stood with a policeman by the door. 'Worked with him at Billingsgate Fish Market!' The throng of reporters were on him at once, all pressing for further details. Clearly flattered by the attention, the old man gave a toothy grin and launched into his story, just as Sergeant Matthews slipped gratefully through a door into a back office. Turning as he did so, he just caught Inspector George Bowman slipping through the reception hall in readiness to climb the stairs to his office.

Bowman's office seemed an oasis of quiet. The hubbub from the ground floor had followed him up the stairs for some considerable distance but here, almost on the top floor, all was calm. Closing the door behind him, he leant against it for a while to catch his breath. Time was he could take those stairs two at a time and not feel any ill effects. Cursing his condition, Bowman moved to the bureau and poured himself a brandy. Having downed the first, he poured another and nursed it in his hand as he walked to the window. The alcohol had calmed him, though he was grateful he had bought himself a pie to line his stomach on the way from Holborn. The afternoon sun was dipping below the adjacent buildings now and Bowman was able to gaze out upon the roofs without squinting. As he allowed his gaze to trace the angles of the tiles his mind turned to the case in hand. Subject to the reports from Doctor Crane at Charing Cross Hospital, it was clear the bodies had met the same end at the same hands. This suggested Alfred Makin was somehow linked to the young lady found in Old Bell Yard and that they both were linked to the murderer. Bowman sunk into his chair. He felt a lot depended on getting an identification for the young lady. With that in hand he could, perhaps, start joining the dots. Draining the glass once more, he placed it on the desk next to him and settled back to give the matter further thought. So it was with some surprise that he was suddenly woken by a knock at the door.

Sitting bolt upright, his heart beating furiously in his chest, Bowman wiped the spittle from his mouth and sprang to the window. Throwing open the sash to admit some air, he quickly placed the glass back on the bureau. Taking a step back from the wall, he turned to face the map that hung there and affected a nonchalant stance. 'Come in,' he said breezily.

The door was flung open to reveal the impressive bulk of Inspector Ignatius Hicks. With pipe in hand and heavy coat trailing to floor, he filled the frame with his vastness. Bowman would often marvel at how such proportions could be housed in one man. As Hicks stretched his arms wide in his customary greeting, there seemed enough of him for two.

'Ah, Bowman,' he boomed. 'I trust I didn't interrupt?' His eyes flitted furtively around the room.

'No, Hicks,' Bowman replied innocently, his attention on the map. 'I was mulling over the details of this morning's find.' Walking to his desk, he opened a drawer. Quickly and guiltily sliding a small hip flask out of view, he reached beyond it in the hope that Hicks hadn't noticed. There he felt a small box. Drawing it out, he snapped the drawer shut and opened the lid. He withdrew two pins and walked back to the map. Tracing the line of High Holborn with a finger, he placed the first in Old Bell Yard, just west of the viaduct. Once placed, Hicks noticed a tiny piece of paper had been affixed to the pin to make a flag.

'This is where the body was found this morning, Hicks. But what of Alfred Makin?'

Hicks marched to the map, trailing smoke in his wake. Making a strange clicking sound with his tongue that Bowman found most distasteful, the portly inspector stabbed at the map with a fat finger. 'There,' he breathed. 'Furnival's Inn.'

Bowman peered closer. So Makin had lain just a few

hundred yards from where the second body had been found. He placed a pin at the point where the alley met High Holborn. 'Step back, Hicks.' As his companion shuffled back to the desk, Bowman joined him to peer back at the wall. 'Of all the streets represented here,' the inspector began, his moustache twitching at his lip, 'our two bodies were found almost a stone's throw away from each other on consecutive mornings.' Hicks nodded in agreement. He could see the tiny flags, turned as they were towards each other, were almost touching. It was a graphic illustration. 'We're after the one man, Hicks.'

'I have news from Doctor Crane,' Hicks said ominously, 'that would confirm it.' He swept past the desk to the window. Smoke billowing from his pipe, he leant his weight against the sash and, to Bowman's consternation, pulled it down as he spoke. 'He has had a cursory examination of the young lady's body.' Bowman's eyebrows rose in expectation. 'Same injuries. The puncturing of the - ' Hicks paused. 'The whatchamacallit.' Bowman frowned. 'The windpipe!' Hicks spluttered, triumphantly.

'Punctured?'

'Oh, yes,' leered Hicks. 'Seems he used force enough to break a bone in the neck.'

'And it would be quick, too.'

'Aside from that, the doctor found nothing but injuries that might be ascribed to a struggle and a fall. Bruising on the fists, cuts to the back of the head, that sort of thing.'

Bowman set his fists on his desk and leant against them. 'But what links them both, Hicks? If only we knew the identity of the second body.'

'It's a Miss Clemmie Porter.' Sergeant Graves stood in the doorway, two large boxes stacked each upon the other in his arms. His curls bounced on his head as he moved to the desk and let go his burden. Bowman marvelled that he should be the only one short of breath after climbing the stairs.

'I took it upon myself to ask around,' Graves continued, rubbing dust from his hands. 'We know she was a flower girl from the basket that lay beside her, so I walked to all their local haunts. I got lucky at Covent Garden.'

'Well done, Graves,' Bowman enthused. 'Is there more?'

'That there is,' Graves continued with a wink. 'She spent her days at Covent Garden but lived just north of High Holborn.' He sat on the desk, swinging his foot absently as he spoke. 'In a hostel off Bloomsbury Court.'

Bowman strode swiftly to the drawer once more, opening it carefully so as not to reveal its contents. Pulling the box of pins from the drawer, he took another flag gingerly between forefinger and thumb and returned to the map.

'Bloomsbury Court,' he murmured as his eyes scanned the narrow streets, back alleys and lanes to the north of High Holborn. 'There.' He stabbed at the map with the pin, planting the flag in a packed row of houses situated where High Holborn forked into Oxford Street and Broad Street.

'And Alfred Makin?'

'Lamb's Conduit Passage,' Graves reminded the inspector. He swung himself from the desk, took a pin from Bowman and placed it just a quarter of an inch from Red Lion Square.

'They lived a good half a mile from each other, with seemingly nothing to connect them. An old soldier and a flower girl,' Bowman's frown cut all the deeper on his forehead as he mulled over the implications. 'And yet they were found within a hundred yards of each other, the other end of High Holborn.'

'Coincidence?' offered Hicks, none too helpfully.

'Perhaps,' Bowman consented. His eyes alighted on the boxes that Graves had placed on his desk.

'Ah!' exclaimed the young sergeant as he followed Bowman's gaze. 'Possessions!' He whipped the lids off the boxes, each some six inches deep and a foot wide, as though he had reached the dramatic denouement to some magic trick.

The detectives crowded round the desk, peering into the piles of possessions and trinkets that lay within the boxes. 'I brought them over from Charing Cross,' Graves twinkled. 'Thought you'd like a look before I put them in the properties store.'

Bowman was reaching gingerly into the box marked 'Makin, A. Strangling, Holborn'. He held up a pair of shapeless trousers, a long-sleeved, collarless shirt and a tatty waistcoat. The poor man's cap lay at the bottom of the box but, as Bowman lifted it, he found it concealed a collection of change, some matches, a full, unsmoked pipe and a pouch of tobacco. There was something calm and almost ritualised in Bowman's movements, Graves noticed. He was clearly alive to the indignity inherent in rifling through a dead man's belongings, but mindful also that something of value might be found there. Hicks, on the other hand, was diving in with little ceremony. Springing to the box marked 'Porter, C. Strangling, Holborn', he fair near upturned the box in his haste to examine its contents.

'A pretty dress,' he leered as he held it up to the light. It was clearly his intention to give a running commentary of his findings to all who would care to listen. 'A coat and bonnet.' A sudden blush came to his cheeks as he peered in deeper. 'Ah,' he spluttered. 'Undergarments.' Graves and Bowman exchanged a look, the former barely suppressing a laugh at the inspector's discomfort. Reaching in to move the offending articles to one side, Hicks pulled out some sundries that lay beneath, resting in the flower lady's basket. 'A hat pin,' he exclaimed needlessly. 'Some coinage, a bundle of lavender.' He made a haphazard pile on the desk. There lay all that was left of a life, thought Bowman sadly. All Clemmie Porter had in the world was now arranged before him, in a little pile. It was with a great sadness that he realised that neither box had included a pair of shoes. Bowman knew such things were a luxury amongst the poor. How on Earth they managed in the depths of winter, he could not fathom. In the meantime, Hicks was lifting an unsmoked cheroot and an exquisite, silver cigarette paper holder from the box.

'Clearly stolen,' he breathed. He was no doubt right. It was certainly questionable whether a woman of such lowly means could afford such an ornate étui. One side had been rubbed almost flat, Bowman noticed, a sign perhaps of just how much she had loved the thing. Hicks teased a small book of Swan papers from the holder, then finally reached back into the box to retrieve a pouch of rolling tobacco. After giving it a hearty sniff, he dropped it with no particular decorum alongside the other items on the desk.

'And that,' he announced, clapping his hands together, 'is that.'

Bowman let his eyes wander over the detritus before him. What stories might these things impart if he could but hear them?

'What are we looking for, sir?' Graves blinked as the afternoon sun reflected off the implacable Thames beneath Bowman's window.

'Anything, Graves, that will provide a link.' Bowman smoothed his moustache absently with a finger. 'If we could but know their last movements we might build a better picture.' Carefully, he picked through the two piles of belongings before him. From the corner of his eye, he noticed Hicks tapping his foot impatiently against the floor.

'I am not entirely sure what a man might learn from the possessions of the deceased,' he harrumphed. Reaching deep into his pocket, he retrieved his pipe and tamped some fresh tobacco down in its bowl. As the rotund inspector struck a match against the sole of his shoe, Bowman took a breath. Graves fancied he could see the pieces falling in his eyes like a puzzle. Reaching to the desk, Bowman fingered Makin's pocket of tobacco. It was tied with a leather lace threaded through several holes at

185

the opening. His fingers shaking more than he cared to admit, he gently untied the cord and opened the pouch. Tipping his hand, he emptied the contents into a tidy heap, using his little finger to shepherd some stray strands back to the pile as they drifted across the desk. They were finely cut and golden brown in colour, and Bowman could smell a heady aroma escaping from the bag as he peered inside.

'Turkish,' announced Hicks with authority through a cloud of his own smoke. 'Common enough.'

Placing the empty pouch to one side, Bowman moved to the pitiful pile of Clemmie Porter's effects. Her pouch was more like a soft leather wallet, closer in design to an envelope. It was embroidered along its fold with grapes on a vine, though these, like the design on the étui, were long since faded. The flap was fastened with a stud that opened with a gentle pop and Bowman again emptied the wallet's contents onto his desk. The same finely cut shreds of tobacco arranged themselves into a neat pile, matching the former in both colour and volume.

'Like I said,' offered Hicks with a shrug. 'Common enough.'

'It is not the brand nor the type that concerns me, Hicks,' said Bowman thoughtfully. 'But the quantity.'

'How d'you mean?' Hicks shifted his enormous weight to lean in closer.

'Is it usual for a smoker to have a full pouch of tobacco?' Bowman's eyes lifted to his companion, seemingly hoping to see his answer writ there in his face.

'Of course!' Hicks laughed. 'If he has just bought an ounce at a tobacconist!' He shrugged as if the import was lost upon him.

Bowman ignored the jibe. 'And how long might an ounce last?'

'Depends,' Hicks expounded, glad to have stumbled into territory upon which he could enlarge with authority. 'I should say an ounce would last me two or three days. A cheroot smoker like your lady there,' he pointed at the tattered dress on the desk, 'Might enjoy an ounce over four or five days.'

'So,' continued Bowman, his eyes narrowing as much in thought as in the face of the smoke from Hicks' pipe, 'it would be unusual to find two random pouches of tobacco that had just been filled?'

'I suppose so, yes.' Hicks was speaking slowly now, trying to keep up with his fellow inspector's train of thought.

Bowman stood. 'Just how much would you say was in those piles, Hicks?'

Hicks applied his practised eye to the small, golden heaps on the table. 'Just about an ounce, I should say. Maybe a touch more.'

'So we may assume they had just purchased a refill from a tobacconist?'

'I dare say. Or, at the least, very recently.'

'What does all this mean, sir?' Graves was shaking his head in confusion.

'I'm not sure, Graves,' Bowman sighed. 'But I feel that detail is of some importance to the case.' He turned once more to the map. 'Inspector Hicks, I think we should take a walk.'

High Holborn was still bustling. Inspectors Hicks and Bowman stood outside The Viaduct Tavern, a grand public house opposite Newgate Gaol occupying a plot on the corner of Newgate Street and Giltspur Street. It rose over four impressive storeys, the upper floors containing rooms for rent to impoverished servicemen. Even through the grime of the street, the plasterwork that defined the balustrades stood in sharp relief against the brick, each window crowned with a neat, white portico. They stood facing west, up and over Holborn Viaduct which lay before them and on to High Holborn.

'We know Alfred Makin spent his last evening here,' Bowman shouted above the clatter of carriages, 'We should retrace his steps to where he met his death.'

Hicks had half an eye on the tavern at Bowman's back. 'Might there be time for a pie before we begin?' Catching sight of a paper seller at his stall, Bowman reluctantly nodded his assent. Far be it from him to stand between an officer of the Metropolitan Police Force and his appetite. As Hicks rubbed his hands in anticipation and made his way into The Viaduct, Bowman crossed to where the paperboy was selling his copies of The Evening Standard.

'Read all about it!' he was crying. 'Holborn Strangler strikes again!' Bowman noticed he had a steady stream of custom. Every third person, it seemed, was eager to feast their eyes on the latest ghoulish goings on described, no doubt in titillating detail. Bowman saw one man gawking with relish at the headline, only to devour the news with as much gusto as Hicks might devour his dinner.

'Evening Standard!' cried the boy as he held a copy aloft.

'I'll take one,' said Bowman as he reached into his pocket for change.

'Reckon they'll catch 'im?' the boy asked, his eyes wide. Bowman paused to regard the slight figure before him. He wore a torn pair of trousers, the hems of which dragged in the dirt about his bare feet. His shirt had, no doubt in some boyish altercation, had the collar ripped from it and a sleeve hung torn to the elbow. His shining face peered out from beneath a cloth cap that only just contained a mop of unruly chestnut hair.

'Oh yes,' Bowman replied as he reached for his copy of The Standard. 'I'm sure they will.'

'Rum of him to escape from under their noses though, weren't it?'

Bowman couldn't help but agree. 'Rum, indeed,' he concurred.

'Ask me,' the boy continued, clearly warming to his theme, 'I'd sack the lot of 'em and start again.'

Bowman could barely contain his mirth. 'Sack whom?' he asked.

'The Scotland Yarders. They ain't got a clue.' He leaned in closer, taking another newspaper from the pile beside him. 'Reckon I could do better meself.'

Stung by the remark, Bowman contented himself with a weak smile and shook the paper open before him. Leaving the lad to his employment, he walked back to the door to the Viaduct Tavern to await Inspector Hicks. He leant against the doorjamb, deliberately angled into the street so as not to be tempted by the pumps and optics on display behind the bar and turned his gaze to the text beneath the sensational headline. 'The Holborn Strangler,' it exclaimed hysterically, 'has claimed another victim on the streets of London! Pretty Clemmie Porter was found in Old Bell Yard, her body left to the rats.' The inspector rolled his eyes. 'The popular flower girl was known to all in Covent Garden and Billingsgate where her fragrant posies were well-sought after.' Bowman blinked and read the line again. Billingsgate. It was the second time he had heard the name of London's most famous fish market in as many hours. Casting his mind back, he recalled the crooked man in the reception hall of Scotland Yard, besieged with reporters at his mentioning having known Hubert Kabble at Billingsgate. Bowman's moustache twitched at his lip. He let the newspaper drop to his side and his mind wander freely down the alleys of his intuition. There was a door closed to him, he knew. As much as he pushed against it, so it remained locked. All his thoughts were converging on a single fact but, try as he might, it eluded him.

'Come on, Bowman,' interrupted Hicks, a steaming pie in his great paw. 'Don't stand on ceremony.' Shaken from his reverie, Bowman turned to face his companion to see rivulets of gravy running from his beard.

'Hicks, we'll proceed west.' Bowman stepped from the pavement, negotiating his way through the traffic that had only increased as the afternoon progressed. Smart carriages jostled for position with speedy traps and cabs, each darting between the other as if in a dance. Gangs of urchins ran between their wheels, reaching up to the wealthier passengers for succour where it could be found. Very occasionally, one would be rewarded with a crust or a handkerchief, for most the reward would be a cuff about the head. Passing over Farringdon Street at quite some height, the viaduct swept over Shoe Lane to Holborn Circus. A hundred yards later, the two men stopped at Prince Albert's statue. Despite the dimensions of the monolith before them, and the exquisite detail in the statue, few of the passersby gave it a thought. Once considered a jewel in Holborn's crown and unveiled by Her Majesty the Queen herself, the statue presented her husband in military dress, whiskered and sideburned. Once it had drawn crowds and stopped the traffic, now all passed by without so much as a glance.

'There is Furnival's Inn,' spat Hicks, looking up the road. 'Where Makin's body was found.'

Bowman followed his gaze. 'I would assume Makin was on his way home when he was attacked.'

'Then he didn't get far,' breathed Hicks in a tone that passed for sentiment.

Bowman nodded in agreement. Glancing absently up High Holborn, his eyes fell upon a building that stood back a little from the road next to a public house beyond Furnival's Inn. A dilapidated building, it stood only by the grace of God it seemed, rather than any structural integrity. It was squat and unimposing, almost apologetic in its aspect. On a sign above the door, in gold lettering that was almost as faded as the picture of a smoking pipe beneath, were two words; 'Culpepper's Tobacco.'

'Come on,' Bowman commanded, dodging behind a carriage in a sudden haste.

'What is it, Bowman?' Hicks protested. 'Can't a man be given a moment to finish his supper?' Puffing wildly, he swung his great frame from the statue where he had been leaning and took his chances amongst the traffic. If he knew that half his pie and its contents were running down the front of his coat, he evidently didn't care.

Culpepper's Tobacco stood between The Three Bells and a ramshackle slum of a building just beyond the junction to Gray's Inn Road. The door was propped open, and Bowman had to stand aside to let three or four customers exit the shop to the road before he entered. Already, he was assailed with the pungent aroma of many blends of tobacco. It wasn't an unpleasant smell by any means. Indeed, Bowman found its heady scent invigorating, far more than the resultant fumes when it was smoked. Removing his hat and bowing his head so as not to crack it on one of the many low beams that spanned the ceiling, he let his eyes wander around the shop's interior to get his bearings. His first impression was one of darkness, but as his eyes grew accustomed to the gloom he saw cabinets and shelves lined with boxes and tins of all sizes. Bowman was sure it had once been a smart establishment. As he peered into the shadows, he could just make out wooden panels proclaiming 'Tobacco is good for you!' and displaying the proud boast that all the produce sold at the shop was 'Genuine Tobacco!'. The signs were faded, their paint chipped and the lettering indistinct. Each cabinet was separated from its neighbour by an ornate pillar, painted with a marble effect and crowned with a decorative capital. The cabinets were glass fronted and, no doubt, had once been clean. Now they were smeared with fingerprints and grime, obscuring the view inside. Bowman reached out and swung the door open to reveal boxes branded with such names as Old Virginia, Bulwark, Doctor's Blend and Wilson & McCallay's Happy Thought. A whole wall of cupboards was given over to the sale of snuff, the taking of which was more commonplace than ever but was a practise that Bowman could not abide. Yet more shelves held boxes of cheroots and cigars. Down the centre of the room ran a long cabinet with several partitioned compartments, each labelled with the name of a different blend. Looking closely, Bowman could see each contained a quantity of shredded or cut tobacco and a small, grubby shovel.

Beside him, Hicks considered each cabinet with the studied air of a connoisseur. Bowman could see him playing with the change in his trouser pocket, intent, no doubt, on making a purchase before their investigations were over.

'May I help you?' The voice was dry and cracked. Taken by surprise at the sound, Bowman turned to see the oddest of men at the counter. Barely over five feet tall and seemingly as round as he was tall, a grubby apron was tied around his waist. His hands fidgeted on the glass-topped counter before him as he spoke. His hair was parted in the centre and slicked down either side of his head to protruding ears. He had a fleshy nose that sprawled across his face and upon which rested the thickest pair of spectacles Bowman had ever seen. The man's eyes were magnified by the lenses so that they seemed to stand out from his face like the stalks of some strange snail. Most remarkable of all, however, was the man's skin that looked for all the world as if it were comprised entirely of tobacco leaves. Even in the half-light it shone as if it had been burnished. The wrinkles around his eyes and on his cheeks seemed like the ribs and veins of the tobacco leaf. In a quite remarkable way, he seemed to be part of the shop, a fixture as much as the cabinets and shelves that lined the walls. When he spoke again, it was with the rasp of a heavy and lifelong smoker. 'Each of the blends in the centre is a penny an ounce.' His lungs seemed to fizz and pop as he breathed.

'I am not here to buy,' Bowman replied. He heard a snort from Hicks at the furthest cabinet. Peering over his shoulder, Bowman could see him fingering his change.

'Then what can I do for you?' The little man looked somewhat confused. Bowman watched him carefully.

'I am Detective Inspector Bowman and this, Detective Inspector Hicks. We are from Scotland Yard.' Impossibly, the man's eyes grew wider still. 'Are you Mr Culpepper? Bowman had moved to the counter now.

The man nodded. 'Aloysius Culpepper, sir,' he gulped. 'And this is my shop. Has been these last thirteen years.' Culpepper shuffled to the front of the shop, gesturing wildly that Hicks should move out of his way. He moved with such a lack of grace that Bowman could not help but wonder that he could walk at all. Indeed, by the time he had reached the door, he was out of breath, though he had only undertaken a journey of a few yards. Swinging the door shut, he bolted it against further custom and leaned against it to catch his breath. 'You'll find my books are in order,' he wheezed. 'I have all the necessary licences and permissions in my office.'

'We are not here to look over your permissions,' chuckled Hicks.

'Not here to buy, nor check my permissions?' Culpepper was rubbing his hands, nervously. Bowman had seen such behaviour before. Even an innocent man was reduced to irrational delusions of guilt in the presence of a Scotland Yarder. 'Then what would you have of me?'

'Only information,' Bowman soothed. He noticed that as he or Hicks spoke, Culpepper would turn his head to search for them in the near darkness. He suspected that, despite the magnificent lenses, the poor man was very nearly blind. It would certainly explain why the shop was so gloomy, for why would a man half blind want light?

'We are investigating the discovery of two bodies over previous nights, here in Holborn.'

In response, the tobacconist let go a great, shuddering cough that seemed to shake the very building. His whole body rattled as he fought for control, coughing again and again into his hand. When he had calmed himself, he wiped his flat palm across his apron and presented Bowman with a smile. 'Go on,' he said as if such an interruption was nothing out of the ordinary. Bowman realised the man could hardly have read about either case.

Hicks leaned in. 'There is a detail that has led us here,

Mr Aloysius Culpepper.'

'Detail?' the man blanched.

Hicks was having too much sport at the poor man's expense, and Bowman shot the portly inspector a warning look. 'Mr Culpepper,' Bowman smiled again. 'We have reason to believe that both our subjects stopped to charge their tobacco pouches before they died.' He was having doubts about the efficacy of his plan even as he continued. 'If we were to furnish you with a description of each of them, might you be able to tell us if they visited your shop in the hours before their deaths?'

As if to confirm Bowman's doubts, Culpepper shook his head. 'Not from their description, no, inspector.' He shuffled back to his counter as he spoke, reaching out to each cupboard and cabinet for support as he passed them. 'My advancing years, I'm afraid, have taken whatever sight I once had. I can see enough to know if I have custom and use my other senses to know if they are trying their luck.'

'How so?' Bowman raised his eyebrows.

'You would be surprised, inspector, just how much noise a hinge will make when a cabinet is opened.' Bowman nodded in admiration. He had heard tell of other senses becoming that much more acute upon the loss of another and had a memory of a blind man in Hampstead who was accounted one of the best piano tuners.

'One was a military man, an Alfred Makin.'

Culpepper was brought up short by mention of the name. 'I know him well enough. He is indeed a regular customer.' He took a breath that seemed to rattle to his boots. 'Is Alfred Makin dead?'

'Makin was found in Furnival's Inn night before last,' Hicks confirmed.

Culpepper's huge eyes blinked in the gloom. 'But that is just across the way.'

'And Clemmie Porter was found this morning but a stone's throw away.'

'Alfred Makin was indeed at the shop the night before last.' Culpepper was trying hard to contain his tears. 'We fought together at Khartoum. He would come in every week to share his tales and recharge his pouch.' He set his face into a mask of defiance. 'If I am guilty of any crime with regard to Alfred Makin, inspector, it is to allow him to take an eighth or so over the ounce at no extra cost.'

'What time did he visit last night?'

'Late,' Culpepper rasped. 'I'd say eleven of the clock. I close my doors at midnight, inspector,' he continued off Hicks' questioning look. 'I need every penny I can make and the late crowds are good for trade.' Suddenly aware of Bowman's eyes upon him, he returned to the matter at hand. 'I served Alfred with an ounce of his usual Turkish.'

Bowman's eyes narrowed. 'And Clemmie Porter? She was a young girl taken last night in a similar way to Makin.'

'There's many a young lady comes in here, inspector,' Culpepper shrugged. 'I could not vouch that any of them are your girl.'

'She was a flower girl from Covent Garden,' Bowman pressed on. 'Might she have talked trade with you?'

'A flower girl, you say?' Culpepper's eyes grew larger

still and his fingers danced in agitation on the counter top.

'Might there be something in that?' Hicks leant on the table, the better to read the tobacconist's face. Bowman was afraid his sheer weight might crack the glass.

'There might.' Culpepper cleared his chest again with a great hacking cough that almost split Bowman's ears. 'There was a girl came in late last night,' he continued. 'Just as I was closing. She might be the one.'

'How can you be sure?' Bowman stroked his moustache as he listened.

'I have come to depend on my other senses since my sight began to fail. I am possessed of a keen sense of hearing and an acute sense of smell.' Bowman heard Hicks harrumph beside him. Culpepper continued, regardless. 'Just as I was closing the door on my night's trade, a young woman asked for an ounce of Turkish. It's a popular enough brand, inspector, so I should not read too much into that. However, her appearance was accompanied by the arrival of a particular scent that I recognised.' Bowman leaned in and even Hicks could not help but be enthralled by the man's account. 'Lavender,' Culpepper exclaimed by way of a denouement. 'The scent was so strong she can only have been carrying a bundle of the stuff.' The tobacconist blinked in the half-light. 'Might she have been your girl?'

Bowman took a breath. He was almost certain in his mind that the girl who had called in on Culpepper last night had indeed been Clemmie Porter. And that soon thereafter, she had been found in the dirt on Old Bell Yard. 'Then they both stopped by your shop before meeting their death.'

'Life is full of coincidences, inspector,' declared Culpepper with a shrug, 'Perhaps there is nothing in it at all.' Bowman nodded, thoughtfully. 'Now,' said Culpepper breezily. 'Is there anything else I might do for you?'

'There is, Mr Culpepper,' leered Hicks. 'You may serve me with an ounce of your freshest Edgeworth Ready Rubbed. And an eighth more for free wouldn't go amiss.'

Bowman stabbed another pin into the map. The little flag marked the location of Culpepper's tobacco shop and was, indeed, just a short walk away from where the two bodies had been discovered. Beside him, Inspector Hicks was stroking his great beard.

'What does that tell us, Bowman, other than where they bought their tobacco?' Hicks looked his fellow inspector up and down. It was clear the stairs had taken their toll upon him and a fine sweat had glazed his brow. Bowman leant against the map while his heart settled. Then, walking suddenly to the window, he threw open the sash to admit some evening air. Closing his eyes against the breeze, he leant on the sill and breathed deep. Although his office was of more than adequate size, he had felt the walls pressing in against him as Hicks had been speaking. Even the ceiling seemed a good six inches lower. A throbbing had settled at his temples. Bowman knew exactly what would calm him, but he also knew that he must wait until he was alone to avail himself of it. He opened his eyes. The River Thames was in full spate below and butted up against the great Victoria Embankment. Gangs of children played amongst the legs of smart businessmen returning home from a day's work and young couples out to take the air. One such pushed a pram before them, stopping only to receive an errant blanket that caught on the breeze and slipped to the ground. One man in particular caught his eye. He was dressed in a formal frock coat and pinstriped trousers and wore a necktie fastened about a wing-collared shirt. A smart top hat sat precariously on his head, and every now and then he would reach up to secure it against the wind. As he reached a tree directly beneath Bowman's window, a sudden thought seemed to occur to the man and he turned, mid-stride, to walk back the way he had come. Shaking his head, the man had evidently forgotten something or realised he should be somewhere else entirely.

'What were they doing so far from their homes, Hicks?'

'They weren't that far at all,' blustered Hicks, pulling his pipe from a pocket. Tapping it against Bowman's desk to release a plug of ash in the bowl, he drew out a leather pouch bulging with tobacco. 'Both their lodgings were but a ten or fifteen minute walk.'

Bowman turned from the window with a clearer head. Looking at the map from a distance, he felt as if the whole of London lay before him. If he looked close enough, he fancied he might just see the citizens of the metropolis going about their business, both lawful and unlawful. How he wished he was afforded such a bird's eye view of the streets outside his window. Criminal misdemeanours, or at least the patterns and movements that attended them, would be the easier to identify. He would be godlike. Fixing his eyes on the location of Culpepper's shop, he walked back to map, forcing himself to focus on the specifics of the case. 'This makes no sense, Hicks,' he said at last. The bluff inspector paused with a match halfway to his pipe, propping himself up against the back of Bowman's wing-backed chair in preparation to hear his companion's thoughts.

'How so?' he asked.

Bowman raised a finger to the map and tapped the position of The Viaduct Tavern with a nail. 'Two nights ago, Alfred Makin took a drink or two in The Viaduct.' Hicks nodded. Bowman traced the course of High Holborn over Farringdon Street and toward Culpepper's shop. 'He then stopped here to buy some tobacco on his way home.' He tapped the map again, this time close to the flag indicating the tobacconist's location.

'All this we know,' boomed Hicks, taking the first draw on his pipe. The match flared as the tobacco caught the flame, and the inspector released great plumes of smoke from his mouth and nostrils, almost completely concealing his face from view.

'Last night, Clemmie Porter made her way from Covent Garden.' Bowman was tracing her journey on the map, up Russell Street and along Broad Street to High Holborn. 'She actually had to walk out of her way to Culpepper's shop.'

'Perhaps she knew it was the only tobacconist's to open so late,' Hicks offered.

'Perhaps,' Bowman concurred. He paused, then took a

breath. 'Why did they not then go home?'

Hicks guffawed as he shook his match to extinguish the flame. 'I should say that was obvious,' he bellowed. 'They were both murdered!'

'They did not go home,' Bowman continued in spite of the interruption and mindful of the smart businessman he had seen from his window, 'because something or someone changed their minds.' Something approaching a thoughtful expression settled on Hicks' face as he considered the implications. 'Otherwise,' continued Bowman, 'why did they not continue on their journey? Alfred Makin to Lamb's Conduit Passage and Clemmie Porter to Bloomsbury Court?' He tapped the two locations with his finger. They both lay on the western approach to New Oxford Street, in the opposite direction to where their bodies had been found. 'Rather than going home after their visit to the shop, both victims decided to head in the other direction entirely.' Bowman turned to face his portly partner, his eyes wide as he posed what he thought to be the most important question of all; 'Why?' The word hung in the air and Hicks chewed on the stem of his pipe. Bowman pressed his point. 'Why were they both heading in the same direction when they were attacked? Away from their lodgings?'

Hicks shifted his great bulk from the back of the chair. His eyes scanning the map, he took the pipe from his mouth and tapped at the streets with the bit. Tracing a line from Culpepper's shop to where each of the bodies had been found, he continued on the journey over Holborn

Circus.

'Let us say they were interrupted in their journeys by their assailant,' he said, slowly. 'Where might they have been going?' His pipe led him over Farringdon Street via the viaduct. As he reached the junction with Snow Hill, he paused. 'Of course, they may have been heading here.' He traced the road to the left and tapped his pipe at a building halfway along the row. Bowman narrowed his eyes to read the legend that had been printed over the property in a plain, uncomplicated font; 'Police Station.'

At that, the door to the inspector's office flew open to admit Sergeant Graves, his eyes full of excitement. 'Sir, I've got more information on Alfred Makin.'

'What is it, Graves?' Bowman was suddenly all attention.

'We knew he'd moved around a bit, picking up what employment he could.' Graves' blond curls bounced on his head as he imparted the news. 'Turns out he spent some time a while back as a porter.'

'Where, Graves?' Bowman had no truck with his companion's propensity to drag out a tale. 'Where?'

Sergeant Graves took a moment to draw his breath, then looked Bowman straight in the eye to deliver the denouement. 'Billingsgate Fish Market.'

The detectives had requisitioned a landau on Whitehall, and the carriage had rattled through the streets to High Holborn at speed. No matter how much his two companions entreated him, Bowman remained stubbornly quiet throughout the journey. The only signs of movement

were in the twitching of his moustache and the slight
tremor that Sergeant Graves noticed in his right hand.
Meeting the sergeant's eyes, Bowman tucked his hand
beneath the other to still it, and directed his gaze outside
to the streets beyond. The air was finally cooling, and he
was grateful for the breeze through the open window. The
low light was taking on a translucent quality, glancing off
the windows to shimmer in the street or dance on the
buildings on the shady side of the road. The crowds were
still numerous, but their intent had changed. Now, instead
of going about their business or walking to their places of
employment, they walked the streets in search of a
diversion. Many cabs were hailed for the theatre district
and the street-side chophouses, gin palaces and pie stalls
threw open their shutters in anticipation of an evening's
trade. The carriage slowed at Holborn Circus, just beyond
Culpepper's Tobacconists and the streets where the two
bodies were found, and its three passengers alighted onto
the dusty road. All around them, Holborn was a bustle.

'You think Culpepper is complicit somehow?' Hicks
blustered, reaching for his habitual pipe.

'Not a bit of it,' breathed Bowman.

'Was he withholding information?'

'None, that I am aware of.' Bowman led his fellow
detectives across the street and in the direction of the
tobacco shop. 'In fact, he was most forthcoming.'

'Then why are we paying him another visit?' Hicks'
exasperation with his companion's methods was almost
comical to see, and Graves allowed himself a smirk at the
inspector's expense. He had long since learned to give

Bowman his head when he had the scent of his quarry.

'Whoever said we were going in?' Bowman asked breezily as the party halted in front of Culpepper's Tobacco.

Glancing through the door, Graves could see the diminutive shopkeeper serving a line of customers, his wide eyes peering through the gloom as he carefully weighed their favourite blend. As the three men turned so their backs were to the shop door, the sergeant took the opportunity to get his bearings. Holborn was not an area he knew well, and he was grateful for the pause in proceedings. Immediately to his left stood The Three Bells, a dingy public house which was full to bursting even at this early hour. Graves could hear a tune being played on a piano and several of the clientele attempting to join in the song. It was not one he recognised. To his right, on the other side of the tobacconist's, stood a rather dilapidated slum. It rose over three storeys, each one in a greater state of disrepair than the one below. Every window had at least a pane of glass missing or cracked, and the brickwork crumbled as if it were chalk. He could see great holes around the windowsills and the door was ill-fitting, as if it had been made for another property entirely. It was secured with a latch that had been tied about with string to fasten it.

'We know that both our victims paid a visit to Culpepper's just hours before they were found,' Bowman was saying, as much for Graves' benefit as anything else. 'In fact, he may well have been the last person to speak to them in life.'

'But you say you do not suspect him?' the sergeant asked.

Bowman turned to the portly inspector at his side. 'Inspector Hicks,' he began, 'if you had just recharged your tobacco pouch at a tobacconist's, what is the first thing you would do on your walk home?'

Hicks shrugged, as if the answer was obvious. 'I would take me first smoke, of course.' He held up his pipe as if by way of illustration.

'Then let us assume Mr Makin and Miss Porter did the same.' Bowman gestured that the two men should give him a little room. They both took a step out onto the pavement to watch the inspector at work. 'They would have exited the shop here, and then both turned right.' Bowman pivoted to face west towards New Oxford Street. 'Mr Makin lived in Lamb's Conduit Passage, Miss Porter at Bloomsbury Court. Both in this direction.'

'This is nothing new!' boomed Hicks, throwing his arms wide. Bowman chose to ignore him.

'Let us assume that they, just as you suggest Hicks, would want to partake of their newly purchased tobacco.' Graves leaned in to follow the inspector's train of thought. 'First, I would say they would move away from the door and start their journey home.' Bowman took a few steps away from the shop. 'Then they would have stopped; Alfred Makin to fill his pipe, Clemmie Porter to roll herself a cheroot.'

Graves nodded. 'Seems reasonable,' he agreed.

'Makin's pipe was full of tobacco when he was found,'

concurred Hicks. 'And Miss Porter's cheroot was found nearby, unsmoked.'

'So, what did they see to make them turn tail?' Bowman looked about him. 'What was it that so filled them with fear that they changed direction entirely, heading back towards the police station on Snow Hill?' The inspector came to rest in front of a grimy window set in the front wall of the ramshackle house behind him. 'Sergeant Graves, you yourself provided me with the last piece of the jigsaw.' Graves raised his eyebrows in response, a smile spreading slowly across his face as Bowman continued. 'I had just read in today's Evening Standard that Clemmie Porter had previously found work at Billingsgate.'

'Alfred Makin had worked there, too!' interrupted Graves, mounting excitement in his voice.

'There was the last piece to the puzzle,' Bowman allowed himself to catch Graves' note of enthusiasm. 'There was our link.'

'I fail to see it,' puffed Hicks.

'Earlier,' began Bowman with increasing urgency, 'I heard at Scotland Yard that Hubert Kabble had worked at Billingsgate Fish Market.'

'The murderer who escaped from Newgate Gaol!' Graves whistled through his teeth at the news, and Hicks took his pipe from his mouth as he considered the implications.

'Mr Culpepper himself said that life is full of coincidences,' continued Bowman. 'But sometimes they are not coincidences at all.'

Graves was piecing together the argument in his mind. 'So Billingsgate was the connection. Both Alfred and Clemmie had known Hubert Kabble.'

'And they would surely have known that he was on the loose again,' Bowman nodded. 'The whole of London is full of the news of his escape.'

'So Hubert Kabble is the Holborn Strangler.' Hicks stood agog at the notion. 'And if they'd seen him,' he eventually continued, 'they would undoubtedly want to alert the authorities. The police at Snow Hill.'

'Unfortunately, Kabble saw them too, and he could not let them live.' Bowman's moustache twitched on his lip.

'But where did they see him?'

Bowman gestured that his two colleagues join him in front of the dilapidated house. As one, they turned to look in at the grimy window. Through the dirty glass, they could each see, sleeping sprawled beneath a pile of filthy rags, a tousled haired, sickly looking man, his mouth hanging open as he snored.

'Kabble!' exclaimed Hicks, inadvertently. The cry was enough to rouse Hubert Kabble from his slumber and he sat up suddenly where he lay, peering through the window to the street beyond.

'Quick, Hicks,' barked Bowman. 'Put your shoulder to that door!'

Hicks was suddenly all action, moving as quickly as his bulk would allow. As Graves kept watch at the window, he saw Kabble spring to his feet, suddenly alert. His fearful eyes rolling in his head, he stumbled from the room, swinging his arms about him in a panic.

'He's getting away, sir!' Graves cautioned. 'There must be a back entrance.'

'There was no back entrance marked on the map,' said Bowman as Hicks pushed his weight to the door. 'He must be heading up and out to the roof. It's the only other way.'

The door gave way in a mess of splinters and dust, and the three men piled into the grotty hallway.

'Hicks!' bellowed Bowman. 'Search the ground floor for any sign of him. Sergeant Graves, come with me.' With a curt nod, Inspector Hicks lumbered into the depths of the house, pulling his revolver from his pocket as he shuffled into the gloom.

Taking the stairs two at a time, Bowman and Graves ascended to the heights of the building. At each floor they came to, they instigated a search of the rooms. Bowman swept his revolver before him in anticipation of catching his quarry but, at each turn, he was denied his opportunity. He was greeted, instead, with such dreadful scenes of deprivation that he had ever seen. In one room, eight men cowered against the far wall, some in a clear state of drug-induced anguish. The others were plainly drunk. Old mattresses and piles of rotting rags littered the floor. There were nearly as many rats in the room as there were men, and two or three scuttled through the inspector's legs as he threw the door open. In another room, three women lay spread-eagled on the floor. Sergeant Graves took a moment to see that they were breathing before gesturing to his superior that they should move on. Finally, they came to the top floor. Having clearly been opened in some haste, a window hung open at a haphazard angle, ripped from its wooden frame. Peering through, Bowman could see the hunched form of Hubert Kabble picking his way carelessly over the tiles. 'Go on, Graves,' commanded Bowman with an acknowledgment that the sergeant was nimbler than he had ever been. 'Get after him, I'll follow.'

Without a moment's hesitation, Sergeant Graves hauled himself through the window and onto the roof beyond. Holding his arms wide for balance, he pursued Kabble amongst the chimney pots and gutters.

'Hold hard, Kabble!' shouted Bowman as he followed. 'There's no escape for you!'

Kabble's voice echoed back. 'There's nothing for me but the noose!' he shouted. Bowman saw him stumble from one roof to the next, reaching out to grab a hold of the brickwork around him. Stooping, he picked a loose tile from beneath his feet and hurled it at Graves. The sergeant ducked as it sailed overhead and crashed through a window behind him. But the action had cost Kabble time. As Bowman held his revolver before him, he saw Graves gaining on the man. The inspector grabbed a pipe to steady himself and looked down the barrel. Kabble was firmly in his sights. Graves had him now, and the two men crashed to the tiles. Rolling on the roof, they exchanged blows and Kabble scratched at Graves' face in desperation. Bowman was upon them now, merely feet away, and he saw Kabble reach behind him for a loose piece of glass that had fallen from a window.

'Graves!' Bowman warned, holding his revolver high. The two men were tumbling so quickly, it was difficult to see which was Graves and which Kabble, and Bowman narrowed his eyes in the anticipation of a clean shot. He saw Kabble raise his arm high and there, in his hand, a shard of glass that cut into his palm. A rivulet of blood ran from his hand and down his forearm to his elbow, but Bowman was more concerned with the sharp point that Kabble had aimed at Graves' face.

'Graves!' Bowman called again. 'Down!'

In the confusion, Graves buried his head in Kabble's chest and Bowman loosed his shot. Kabble screamed in agony as the bullet sliced through the palm of his hand and he dropped the glass shard to the floor. Rolling back in his agony, his head smashed against the loose tiles beneath him and the roof gave way. Graves just had time to prise the man's fingers from his lapels and watch him as he fell, a look of utter surprise on his face, to the floor beneath. And there stood Inspector Hicks. Brushing the dust from his coat, Hicks looked up through the hole in the roof to see Inspector Bowman and Sergeant Graves peering down at him. Clamping his pipe between his teeth, he placed a heavy boot on Kabble's chest.

'Nice of you to drop in,' Hicks chuckled, triumphantly. Catching the look of despair that passed between his colleagues, the bluff inspector scooped Kabble up by the lapels and marched him from the room.

Printed in Great Britain
by Amazon